Cookie Chronicles BOOK FOUR

BEN YOKOYAMA AND THE COOKIE THIEF

THE COOKIE CHRONICLES

Ben Yokoyama and the Cookie of Doom

Ben Yokoyama and the Cookie of Endless Waiting

Ben Yokoyama and the Cookie of Perfection

Ben Yokoyama and the Cookie Thief

Ben Yokoyama and the Cookies of Chaos

WITHDRAWN

Cookie Chronicles BOOK FOUR

BEN YOKOYAMA AND THE COOKIE THIEF

BY MATTHEW SWANSON & ROBBI BEHR

ALFRED A. KNOPF
NEW YORK

THIS IS A BORZOI BOOK PUBLISHED BY ALFRED A. KNOPF

Visit us on the Web! rhcbooks.com

Educators and librarians, for a variety of teaching tools, visit us at RHTeachersLibrarians.com

Library of Congress Cataloging-in-Publication Data is available upon request.
ISBN 978-0-593-43296-9 (trade) — ISBN 978-0-593-43297-6 (lib. bdg.) — ISBN 978-0-593-43298-3 (ebook)

The text of this book is set in 14-point Bembo.
The illustrations were created using Adobe Photoshop, combining digital linework with hand-painted watercolor washes.
Interior design by Robbi Behr

Printed in the United States of America
September 2022
10 9 8 7 6 5 4 3 2 1

First Edition

To Dahlia, Dahna, Darran, and DJ,
for working so hard to balance the scales

The SCHOOLYARD

HOOPS CLUB

ANTI-CLUB CLUB (FOUNDING CHAPTER)

WHEELBARROW CLUB

OTHER HOOPS CLUB

WIZARD CLUB

UNOFFICIAL AD HOC HOPSCOTCH CLUB

CARTWHEEL CLUB

SCHOOL BUILDING

JUNIOR KICKBALL CLUB (KINDERGARTNERS ONLY!)

CLUB PLANNING CLUB

NONCOMPETITIVE CONVERSATIONAL WALKING CLUB

JUST KIDS (NOT A CLUB)

COMICS CLUB

CLUB SANDWICH CLUB

ANTI-CLUB CLUB SPLINTER GROUP

FOUR SQUARE COURT/KID COURT

CHAPTER 1

Ben Yokoyama scooted glumly down the sidewalk with a *thump thump thump*.

He was mad enough that stubbing his toe would have taken him all the way to furious. But he wasn't *quite* mad enough to stop and kick an unsuspecting tree.

He was mad because he was out of almond kisses. He was mad because he had no money to buy more. But mostly he was mad because the chunk of rubber missing from the rear tire of his scooter made an awful *thump thump thump* as he scooted down the sidewalk in dismay.

Ben sighed in a way that was meant to be heard and admired. But no one was close enough to appreciate it.

He sighed louder. But the sidewalk remained empty. Not being able to share his mad feelings made Ben madder.

When he got to the corner with the yellow bush, Ben's best friend, Janet, was waiting with her skateboard.

I heard that sigh a mile away, Ben. What's the problem?

asked Janet.

Ben didn't answer. He wanted Janet's sympathy to last a little longer.

2

"Still mad about those scooter scuffs?"

Ben nodded.

"My skateboard's scuffed, too," Janet pointed out. It was sort of true. "Your skateboard is scuffed in a cool way," said Ben. "My scooter is scuffed in an embarrassing way."

"Why don't you get a new one?" Janet asked.

A new scooter was all Ben wanted. He wanted a new scooter more than he wanted air, and Ben liked breathing a lot. "New scooters are expensive," he argued.

"I thought you got some money for your birthday. You went on and on about how much your aunt gave you."

"It wasn't *that* much," Ben insisted.

"How much was it?"

Ben didn't want to say. A lot of money seemed like less when it was gone.

"Enough for a new scooter?" Janet prodded.

Ben let his face do the talking so his mouth wouldn't have to.

"I see," she said. "What did you spend it on?"

Ben wanted Janet to stop talking about the money he no longer had.

"Almond kisses?"

Ben continued to say no words.

"From Mama Mia's Bakery?"

Ben fiddled with his scuffed handlebar.

"I hope they were delicious," Janet continued. "Were they delicious at least?"

Ben's hungry stomach got fed up with his stubborn brain and forced his weary mouth to surrender the truth.

They were the greatest and the best.

"Well, that's a relief," Janet replied. "Life's too short to eat undelicious cookies."

"Yeah," Ben said wistfully. Janet was right. She usually was.

"So you spent *all* your money, then?"

Ben nodded.

The past tense is the worst.

I'll tell you what, Ben.

Janet dug into her pocket.

I have three dollars, if it helps.

Ben was touched. This was the kind of friend Janet was. He summoned a smile and took the money and tucked it into his coat pocket for safekeeping. Three dollars was better than none. But it wasn't *enough*. A new scooter cost so much more.

Janet hopped back on her skateboard and glided smoothly down the sidewalk as Ben *thump thump thump*ed behind her in scuffed silence.

When they got to the junction of Queen Street and High, they stopped by the front window of Honeycutt Cycle and Scooter. There it was, proudly displayed in all its gleaming glory.

The Astrostar offers a nonslip titanium deck.

Ben had memorized the list of features.

It sports wear-resistant, shock-absorbing wheels, and its best-in-class ceramic bearings ensure the smoothest ride.

"I have to admit, it sounds pretty good," said Janet.

Ben looked at the price tag and thought about his birthday money. It would have been enough. But the Astrostar hadn't come out until *after* Ben's stomach and Mama Mia's almond kisses had cemented their beautiful friendship.

Ben didn't want to regret eating so many.

He didn't want to have to choose between the fleeting joy of almond-kissed delight and the lasting satisfaction of an unscuffed scooter.

He wanted it all. But that was not the way things worked.

It just wasn't fair.

As Ben scooted and scowled and *thump thump thump*ed down the sidewalk, he settled in for a lifetime of disappointment.

The first next step of his regrettable future was school.

CHAPTER 2

Ben liked school. He liked to
learn. He liked seeing his
friends. And he liked playing
kickball at recess.

But as he stood there waiting for the bell, he didn't have the heart to listen as Kyle and Lang argued over who could kick the kickball highest. He didn't have the patience to ask what new huge words Walter had learned or to say nice things about Darby's latest gymnastics trick.

What's *wrong* with you?

asked Janet impatiently.

Ben wasn't sure what to say. His mad had turned to sad. Sad was for sitting down, so he sat on a bench and sighed again, daydreaming that a careless millionaire might wander by and drop a gold nugget at his feet.

Janet shook her head and walked over to chat with Kamari, who was chatting with Darrow and Beckett. Ben sat and sighed and glanced around. Everyone else was smiling and laughing like it was the greatest day in history, which made Ben all the more miserable and hopeless. He needed comfort. He needed

WISDOM.

Then it hit Ben: he knew an
easy way to get both!

He opened his backpack
and found his lunch bag. He
reached inside and pulled
out his fortune cookie.

It caught the attention of Janet, who marched
over with the anxious expression of someone
about to witness a terrible accident. "What's
going on here, Ben?"

He ignored her and started to remove the
clear plastic wrapper from the cookie. A tiny part
of his brain knew he was making a mistake.

"Put the cookie down, Ben," Janet urged with the panicky tone of someone trying to soothe an angry badger. "For your own safety."

Ben had a vague sense that she was right, but it was already too late. He had unleashed a chain of events with such force and momentum that not even a Janet could stop them.

Ben held the cookie up to his nose and took a deep sniff.

"Think of the consequences, Ben!"

But consequences were something that happened *later*. Ben was more concerned with right *now*.

He closed his eyes and savored the immediate future.

Ben anticipated the satisfying crack as the cookie broke open. The flood of flavor as he popped it in his mouth. The thrilling surge of wisdom as he read the fortune it contained. The cookie would know how to make him feel better. It always did.

Ben felt a whoosh as soft as a whisper.

WHOOOOOOOSH

Suddenly the weight of the cookie
disappeared from his hands, as if it had been
lifted by the wind or stolen by an angel.

Ben opened his eyes and immediately wanted
to close them again.

What he saw was not okay.

CHAPTER 3

First Ben saw the feet
and then the teeth.
And then he felt the
menacing glare.
His cookie was
gone. The questions
were why, how, and
who? The answers
were perfectly clear.
Flegg was standing
there, holding Ben's
cookie. Flegg
McEggers. Tall,
strong, and
terrifying.

Flegg was in
fifth grade, outweighed
Ben two to one, and was
approximately eighteen inches
taller. Everyone was afraid of
Flegg. Because Flegg
was the *worst*.

Ben even had a special set of Flegg-related rules:

#1

Always know exactly where Flegg is.

and

#2

Always keep tasty treats hidden from view.

Now Ben had made the double mistake of closing his eyes *and* flaunting his cookie.

The only person who wasn't afraid of Flegg was Janet.

Whatcha doing there, big guy?

she asked, waving her
arms to get his attention.

How about giving
Ben's cookie back?

Janet was trying to sound casual and cool, but
Ben knew it wouldn't work.

"Why?" Flegg seemed genuinely confused, as
if Janet were suggesting he shave off one of his
eyebrows. "It's in *my* hand now."

"Right, but it belongs to Ben," Janet explained,
a little worked up, but not yet
hopping mad.

Ben's heart
pounded and his
stomach clenched.
He felt sick and
scared and ashamed.

He wished *he* were
the one standing up to Flegg
instead of sitting there wilting
like an unwatered plant . . .
but Janet was so much
better at it.

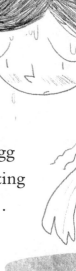

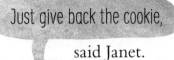

Just give back the cookie, said Janet.

It isn't yours.

But I want to eat it, Flegg reasoned.

GIVE. IT. BACK!

shouted Janet, lunging for the cookie like a chipmunk lunges at a grizzly bear. But Flegg held the cookie high above his head, where Janet couldn't reach it.

"What *is* it, anyway?" Flegg asked, examining the cookie carefully.

"It's just a cookie. It's not even that tasty," Janet insisted.

Flegg held the cookie right in front of his face. "It doesn't *look* like a cookie. But it *smells* like one."

Flegg opened his mouth. Ben saw what was about to happen. He had to act now, or all would be lost.

"Wait!" he shouted. "You can't just *eat* it. There's a piece of *paper* inside."

Stop trying to trick me.

Flegg scowled.

I'm not stupid.

Flegg looked down at Ben like a tower looks down at its shadow.

"Ben's telling the truth!" said Janet, holding up her hands to show she meant no harm. "I know it sounds strange, but inside that cookie is a tiny strip of paper that gives you advice."

"That is the weirdest thing I've ever heard." Flegg seemed ever-so-slightly curious.

"You're not wrong," Janet admitted. "But . . . here's the thing . . ."

Ben could see the sprig of an idea sprouting in her magnificent mind.

Whatever the fortune says *comes true*! For example, that one might say "Stealing is wrong, so give Ben his cookie or else you'll get hit by an asteroid."

It doesn't say that,

said Flegg in a way that seemed ever-so-slightly concerned.

"But it *could*," Janet insisted. "Who do you think would win in a fight between you and an asteroid, Flegg?"

Ben wasn't sure the answer was clear.

"Or . . . ," Janet continued. "What if it says 'People wearing purple pants will get eaten by a tiger today'?"

Ben hadn't noticed, but Flegg's pants were purple.

How does the cookie know what color my pants are?

Flegg asked,
his eyes wide.

"The cookie knows *everything*," said Janet in a sinister whisper, as if sharing a delicious secret. "It peeks into your soul and gives you *exactly* the advice you need."

You're not making sense,

said Flegg.

I never follow advice.

Ben believed it.

"It sounds to me like maybe you're not really interested in the fortune?" Janet prompted.

"Not really," said Flegg, as if they were discussing an extremely rotten egg.

"That's great," said Janet. "How about *you* keep the cookie and *Ben* takes that pesky fortune off your hands?"

Flegg's scowl relaxed as he considered his options. For just a moment, a door opened inside him, maybe wide enough to sneak a cookie through.

What do you say, Ben?

Janet asked, nodding vigorously to steer Ben toward the right answer.

Don't you think you can *share* with Flegg?

Ben was torn. He glanced around. Everyone was watching. Everyone was waiting to see what he would do next. Ben appreciated that Janet was trying to help him, but it wasn't okay for Flegg to keep pushing him around. He needed to prove it to everyone. And to himself.

"I'd . . . prefer to have the fortune *and* the cookie, if you don't mind."

Flegg looked wounded. His open door slammed shut, and the brutal expression returned. "That's not very generous of you."

"It really isn't," hissed Janet, shooting Ben a blistering scowl. "I'm doing my best here, Ben!"

Actually, *I* want both things,

Flegg declared, suddenly realizing he had absolutely no reason to compromise.

If I have to, I can take my purple pants off.

Ben watched with HORROR as Flegg broke the cookie open.

Look, there's a piece of paper inside!

Flegg announced gleefully.

Yes, that's the fortune,

said Janet with exasperation.

That's what we've been talking about.

It's so tiny!

Flegg was extremely pleased.

Tiny and *dangerous,*

Janet reminded him.

This is your last chance to save yourself by giving it to Ben. Then you can eat your cookie and be on your way.

I'm going to tear it up. That way the asteroid can't get me.

WAIT!

said Ben, jolted from his petrified stupor.

First just tell me what it says.

The fortune was a shred of precious wisdom. Ben couldn't live with the thought of never knowing what it said.

Ben's desperate tone must have touched some speck of humanity deep within the heart of Flegg. He blinked at Ben and then squinted down at the fortune.

"It says . . ."

The best things in life are free.

It took a moment for the wisdom to claw its way from Flegg's lips to Ben's embattled brain, but once it landed, Ben's sadness zoomed away like spring arriving on a sudden breeze and vanquishing the darkest winter.

All his problems were solved!

The Astrostar was the *best* scooter. And now it was *free*!

Mama Mia's almond kisses were the *best* treat! And now he could have as many as he liked *without paying a penny*!

Ben didn't need the cookie itself. With this fortune, he'd get everything he'd ever wanted.

I'll share!

he said, leaping to his feet.

You can keep the cookie, Flegg. I'll take the fortune!

No way. Flegg frowned.

I like it. It's *mine.*

He popped the cookie into his mouth with one hand and shoved the fortune deep into his pocket with the other. "Mmmm," he said. "That's *goooooood.*"

He smiled a smile that hit Ben like a bazooka blast, then turned and walked away with great booming strides toward another group of kids who weren't paying quite enough attention.

"And *stay* out!" Janet yelled. It was what Bigger Llama always said when she'd managed to chase the pesky emus out of the roller rink in their favorite show, *Snooptown.*

But Flegg didn't even look back. As he Flegged his way across the grass, kids scattered like there was a force field around him.

Which, in a way, there was.

Flegg was Flegg. He always had been. He always would be. And there was absolutely nothing you could do about it.

CHAPTER 4

"Good riddance," said Janet once Flegg was gone.

Ben said nothing. He couldn't find the right words. He was mad again, but also rattled and embarrassed. He looked around to see who'd noticed, but the answer was *everyone*. He knew because the moment he tried to make eye contact, *everyone* looked away, pretending like it hadn't even happened.

"Good job, Janet," said Janet. "Thanks for sticking up for me, Janet."

Ben was caught between feeling grateful for what she had done and disappointed that it hadn't really worked. "Thanks for trying," he said. "But my fortune is gone."

Janet looked confused. "Maybe Flegg has the paper, but you *heard* the fortune, so you still *have* it, right?"

"A fortune can only belong to one person," Ben insisted. "That fortune was mine, and Flegg stole it. Now *he's* going to get the free stuff."

Ugh. It doesn't say

The best things in life are free to the person holding this piece of paper.

It doesn't work like a gift card, Ben!

"That doesn't make any sense," Ben argued. "If everything was free for everyone, all the stores would go out of business."

"*Exactly*. So why do you deserve to be treated any differently?"

"Because it's *my* fortune!"

"Ugh," said Janet again. "Fortunes don't give you special powers, Ben. They're just words

"That's not what you said to Flegg! You told him whatever the fortune says comes true!"

"I was trying to *trick* Flegg into giving your fortune back because I know how much you love them. You might not have the fortune itself, but you still have the wisdom."

"You really don't think the piece of paper matters?" Ben was hopeful.

"I don't. Plus, I'm pretty sure Flegg is only interested in cookies."

Janet seemed convinced. Ben felt relieved. "Great, then I can finally get my Astrostar."

"What do you mean?" Now Janet was suspicious.

Ben sighed. For the smartest person he knew, Janet could sometimes miss obvious points.

The Astrostar is the *best* scooter.

The best things in life are free.

So, according to my fortune, I can get it for free!

Janet looked at Ben like a jumbo jet looks at a paper airplane.

Ben Yokoyama, do you honestly think people are going to start giving you things for *free*?

That's what the fortune says!

Janet folded her arms and squinted at Ben. "*I* think it says the opposite."

"What do you mean?"

"I think it says to look for things that are already free. And that those things are the *best*."

"That's ridiculous."

"Is it? What about this?" Janet bent over and picked up a pinecone.

"It's a pinecone."

"It's also mysterious and wonderful. The scales are arranged in a Fibonacci sequence. As you know, that's incredible! And pinecones are *free*!"

Ben couldn't disagree. Their teacher, Mr. P., had explained the miracle of pinecones, and Ben was definitely amazed. But Janet was missing the bigger point.

"I agree pinecones are mysterious and wonderful," said Ben. "But they aren't the *best* things. You can't scoot down the sidewalk on a pinecone. You can't eat it for an afternoon snack. Do you have any *other* examples?"

Janet thought about it for maybe two seconds.

"Library books. Bottle caps, avocado pits, blanket forts, spiderwebs, river stones," she said with a delighted smile. "The possibilities are endless, really."

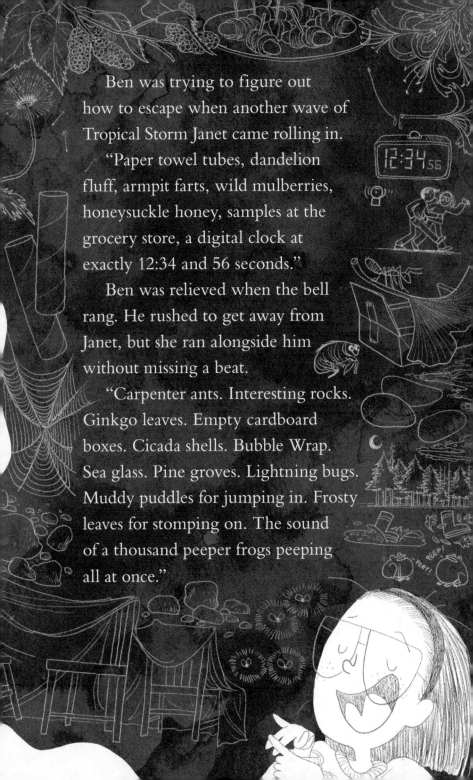

Ben was trying to figure out how to escape when another wave of Tropical Storm Janet came rolling in.

"Paper towel tubes, dandelion fluff, armpit farts, wild mulberries, honeysuckle honey, samples at the grocery store, a digital clock at exactly 12:34 and 56 seconds."

Ben was relieved when the bell rang. He rushed to get away from Janet, but she ran alongside him without missing a beat.

"Carpenter ants. Interesting rocks. Ginkgo leaves. Empty cardboard boxes. Cicada shells. Bubble Wrap. Sea glass. Pine groves. Lightning bugs. Muddy puddles for jumping in. Frosty leaves for stomping on. The sound of a thousand peeper frogs peeping all at once."

She stopped just outside their classroom door with the satisfied look a magician gives at the end of a trick.

But Ben didn't feel like clapping. "Anything else?" he asked sarcastically.

Janet looked Ben straight in the eye.

"As a matter of fact, there is one other great thing I haven't mentioned. *You,* Ben. So far, at least, you have not asked me to pay for the pleasure of your company."

Without waiting for Ben's response, Janet whooshed into the classroom, leaving him to endure the infuriating compliment.

Ben thought about his fortune. He was sure his interpretation was right and Janet's was wrong.

It wasn't that the things she had mentioned weren't great. They absolutely were. But they were all things Ben already *had* or could easily get. He wanted the best things that were hard to come by.

Otherwise, a fortune really *was* just a piece of paper. Ben didn't want to live in a world where that was true.

CHAPTER 5

Ben tried not to think about the best things while his teacher, Mr. P., talked about the three branches of government.

He tried not to imagine scooting smoothly down the sidewalk or munching mountains of almond kisses, while Mr. P. explained how the

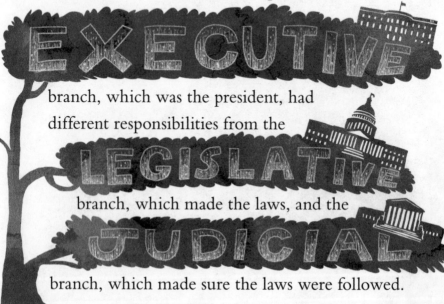

EXECUTIVE

branch, which was the president, had different responsibilities from the

LEGISLATIVE

branch, which made the laws, and the

JUDICIAL

branch, which made sure the laws were followed.

Ben tried to pay attention, but the things he wanted all rushed to the top of his mind like fish farts rise to the surface of a lake.

Ben wished he had the actual fortune to hold and read and place beneath his pillow at night. But Janet had promised that the paper didn't matter, and Ben needed to believe it.

At lunch, Lang had two cupcakes, which was surprising. He usually had one.

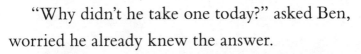

I always bring two, but Flegg usually takes one before I sit down,

Lang explained.

"Why didn't he take one today?" asked Ben, worried he already knew the answer.

"He told me he had to save his appetite. He said later today he's going to get as many cupcakes as he wants . . . for *free*."

That's weird, said Kyle.

How's he going to do that?

Ben didn't want to say.

39

Instead, he looked over to the table where Flegg usually sat with the big pile of things he'd collected from other people's lunches. But today his tray was empty. He was sitting there reading the fortune, over and over again.

Somehow, Flegg must have known Ben was looking. He turned his head and leered at Ben with an awful, gloating grin.

Janet had been wrong. Flegg definitely understood the fortune's power and was planning to use it.

Ben needed to find a way to stop him. He scoured his brain, and way in the back, he unearthed an exciting idea.

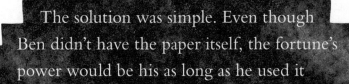

The *first* person to cross the finish line won the gold medal. The *first* person at the dessert table got the biggest piece of cake.

The solution was simple. Even though Ben didn't have the paper itself, the fortune's power would be his as long as he used it

FIRST.

CHAPTER 6

When the final bell rang, Ben raced from the classroom and down the hall, technically walking so he wouldn't get stopped for breaking the no-running rule but walking so quickly he was the first one to the bike rack.

Ben glanced over his shoulder. There was Flegg, leaving the school and heading his way like a distant tornado surging steadily nearer.

Ben's heart lurched, and his fingers tingled with fear. He grabbed his scooter and scooted. Wherever Flegg was headed, Ben had to get there *first*.

After a few *thump thump thump*ing blocks of sweaty effort, Ben glanced back again. Flegg was far behind, moving slowly. Ben took a moment to catch his breath.

THUMP THUMP THUMP THUMP

He'd stopped beside a shop that sold wallpaper. He considered going inside and requesting a roll, just to make sure he used the fortune *first,* but Ben wanted his Astrostar *now.*

As he scooted along, Ben thought, *Soon I'll be rid of you,* thump thump thump. *Soon I'll hear nothing but the silky-smooth whir of my Astrostar.*

Ben imagined how wonderful it would feel to ride one. He could practically *hear* the silky-smooth whir. The daydream felt so vivid and the whirring seemed so real that Ben turned to look. Flegg was right behind him—riding an Astrostar!

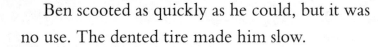

You need a new scooter,

said Flegg with disgust before surging ahead and rounding the corner.

Ben scooted as quickly as he could, but it was no use. The dented tire made him slow.

When Ben turned onto High Street, Flegg was nowhere in sight. His hopes lifted a little. Maybe Flegg had gone home. Maybe Ben still had time to be *first*.

He *thump*ed down the sidewalk to Honeycutt Cycle and Scooter. He flew through the door and rushed to the counter.

One Astrostar, please!

he said between great gulping breaths.

The clerk smirked.

Just *one*? I've seen you out there drooling over it. Are you sure you don't want two or three?

"Just one," Ben repeated. He knew the clerk was trying to be funny, but Ben was in no mood to laugh. Every second mattered.

"You've made a fine choice," said the clerk. "The Astrostar offers a nonslip titanium deck and ceramic bearings that—"

"I know all about it already," said Ben, hoping he didn't sound rude but realizing he probably did. "Could you . . . *hurry,* please?"

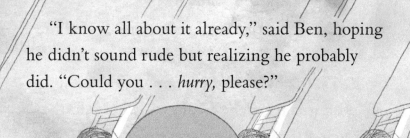

Sure thing,

said the clerk, raising his eyebrows as he walked over to a shelf and brought down a beautiful black box with the word

Astrostar

embossed in shiny golden letters. Ben shivered with anticipation.

"Finally saved enough money, huh?" said the clerk as he placed the box on the counter.

Ben felt panicky at the mention of money. He'd figured the clerk would just hand him the Astrostar and tell him to have a nice day.

Ben thought maybe the clerk just needed a nudge in the direction of the fortune. "This is the *best* scooter you have, right?"

"Absolutely. Did I mention the titanium deck?"

"If it's the *best,* that means it's *definitely . . .*" Ben nodded as he spoke, trying to blaze a trail to the beautiful kingdom where scooters were free.

But the clerk didn't seem to get the hint. "It's definitely *durable,* but it's also quite *stylish.*"

"And also, it's . . . you know . . . *it's . . .*"

I can't think of anything else, kid. I know you're gonna love it.

The clerk made a face like a question mark.

Will you be paying with cash?

46

Ben was devastated. Now he knew for *sure*. Flegg had used the fortune first.

Unless . . . Ben grasped for any fleeting possibility . . . maybe the clerk needed to *hear* the fortune before it would work?

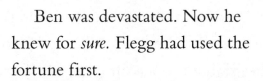

Ben mumbled under his breath in one long caterpillar of wriggling syllables.

What's that?

The clerk leaned in and wrapped his hand around his ear, as if trying to scoop up the sound.

I didn't hear you.

"The Astrostar is the *best* scooter," said Ben, collecting himself. "And . . . well, maybe you haven't heard, but the *best* things in life are . . . *free,*" he said, a bit louder this time.

"Wait. Are you saying I should *give* it to you?" The clerk was grinning now. Ben thought that was a pretty good sign.

"Yes, sir."

"For . . . *free?*"

Ben nodded, his hope on the rise. Maybe talking things through was part of how the fortune worked. "If you're okay with that."

The clerk let out a gleeful giggle that gave way to a jagged chuckle before erupting into a deep and rolling belly laugh that built on itself like a bonfire when the wind blows.

HEY, JIMMY.

A tall teenager shuffled his way across the store and stood slouching next to the clerk with an expression as pleasant as uncooked ham on a cold plate.

Yeah?

This kid expects me to *give* him an Astrostar because . . . *the best things in life are free!*

The clerk unleashed a gusty blast of sputtering guffaws.

Jimmy didn't laugh. Nor did he smile. He stood there blinking as the clerk slapped the counter and laughed so hard that Ben worried he might lose an eyeball.

HA HA HAHAHA HA HAHAWHOOPSSS

Eventually, Jimmy shuffled back to the other side of the store and continued changing the tube on someone's bike.

Ben could feel his face flush red and his forehead get sweaty. He forced his feet to walk through the door and out to the sidewalk, where his old scooter waited in a shameful heap of scuffed sadness.

Ben looked across the street. There was Flegg, just coming out of the Deep Freeze holding a

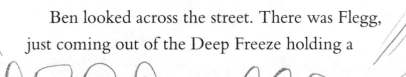

MEGA MEGA

an extremely
expensive ten-scoop
sundae with three bananas,
six cherries, and a river of
hot fudge. Janet and Ben had
several times failed to finish one
together. The Mega Mega was *exactly*
the sort of thing you'd order if you were
twice the size of a typical human and
could get what you wanted
for free.

Now Ben knew for sure
that Flegg had used the fortune first.

Ben wanted to mutter and mope and hide in a hole, but his curious brain got the better of his heavy heart.

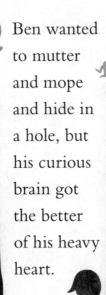

Had the clerk just *handed* the Mega Mega to Flegg? Or did Flegg have to show him the fortune first? These were the sorts of details that mattered to Ben.

He hid behind a minivan and watched the Mega Mega disappear, one gigantic bite at a time. He waited as Flegg hopped back onto his Astrostar and whirred down the sidewalk.

And then Ben crossed the street and opened the door to the Deep Freeze.

"Hey, Ben," said Sammy, the owner, who was throwing away a banana peel. "It's been a while."

Ice cream made Ben's teeth cold, so he didn't eat it often. But Sammy still knew him pretty well.

"What can I get you today?"

"I'm all out of money," said Ben. It wasn't quite true. Janet's three dollars were enough to buy a child-size cone, but Ben's dreams were so much bigger now.

I have a question about the boy who was just in here. Did you . . .

Ben wasn't quite sure how to put it.

Did you give him that ice cream for *free*?

Sammy made a strange face.

Of course not, but . . . weirdly, he *did* try to pay with a fortune cookie fortune.

Ben's eyes got wide.

And then what happened?

I told him we only take actual money.

And then?

He stood there looking really disappointed.

And then?

He paid for his ice cream and left.

Ben was excited! The fortune hadn't worked for *Flegg*, either! But why *hadn't* it? Ben wanted to *understand*!

"Were you . . . *tempted* to give it to him for free?"

"Nope." Sammy was confused. "*Should* I have?"

"Definitely not. Are you tempted to . . . give *me* one for free?"

Sammy shook his head and then glanced around like he was looking for a hidden camera. "*Should* I be?"

"I guess not," said Ben. "I was just hoping you would."

I get it. Free ice cream. That's the *dream,* man.

"Right," said Ben with the disappointed sigh of someone whose sweet dream has just been shattered by a jangling alarm clock.

He went outside and stared at the sky. The answers he sought were not written in the clouds.

NO ANSWERS HERE

Next Ben looked inward, but the view was just as murky. He hadn't gotten his free scooter, and Flegg hadn't gotten his free Mega Mega. What was going on?

"This is all your fault," said Ben to his scooter. He longed to throw it into a volcano, but he didn't know where to find one. Instead, he hopped on and began his long, miserable, *thump*ing ride home.

CHAPTER 7

Ben *thump thump thump*ed to Janet's house and knocked on the door. It opened immediately, but only a little.

"I've been waiting for you," said Janet, peeking out. "I have something that's going to cheer you up."

Ben doubted it.

She opened the door the rest of the way and raised both of her arms like a referee does when someone kicks a field goal.

TA-DA!

Janet was wearing the most astonishing coat Ben had ever seen. It was like a cape and a bathrobe and a Bigfoot all in one.

What do you think?

While Ben stood there trying to form a question that would fit the shape of his surprise, Janet went ahead and answered it.

"I went to the thrift store on the way home from school and found this. It called to me, Ben."

Janet danced around the room as she spoke.

The price tag said $10.00, and I offered her $5.00. Then she offered me $7.50, and I said, "Not a penny more than $2.50!"

Janet was acting out the negotiation with dramatic twirls and bows. Ben wondered if she'd recently eaten some candy.

At which point, I could tell she was starting to crack. She offered me $4.00. I squinted and offered her $1.00.

Ben figured Janet was just about done. But he was mistaken.

"So she offered me $2.00, and I politely said no and marched out of the store. Was I disappointed? Somewhat, but I was all out of money, since I gave my last three dollars to you."

Janet stood there waiting for Ben to ask what happened next. He didn't want to ask, but she kept waiting, and things got awkward, so Ben gave up and grudgingly mumbled, "What happened next?"

"You'll never believe it!" Janet exclaimed. "She followed me out of the store and admitted she'd been trying to get rid of the coat for months because it took up so much room on the rack *and* because it had made a little kid cry. And then she begged me to take it . . . for *free*!"

Ben said
nothing. He
had nothing
to say.
"For free, Ben!
I can't decide
whether to call it Coatzilla
or Coat Kong."
Ben buried his face in his hands.
"But I haven't even shown you the best
part yet. The best part of my day, or maybe
my entire week."

Ben didn't want to hear about the best part
of Janet's day. He was still focused on the worst
part of his.

Look!

Janet's enthusiasm
yanked Ben back from
the depths of his
misery. When he
glanced up again, she
was wearing sunglasses
so huge they blocked
out most of her face.

Ben actually yelped. The sunglasses were *that* upsetting. His brain was spinning with questions.

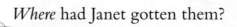

Where had Janet gotten them?

How had she acquired them?

And, most important, *why*?

Ben didn't have to ask. Janet was a blender at top speed.

"I was walking past Mr. Hoggenweff's house. He was out in his yard, trimming his perfect hedge, wearing these incredible sunglasses. I told him how spiffy he looked. I wish you could have seen his face. He was very surprised."

Mr. Hoggenweff was the least pleasant person Ben had ever met. He assumed it was the first time Mr. Hoggenweff had been called "spiffy" in his entire life.

"He told me, and I'm not even kidding, that he didn't *like* the sunglasses. He was *forced* to wear them because he was recovering from cataract surgery, and he was 'darn tired' of them. And then . . . *he threw them across the yard*!"

Ben considered this an appropriate reaction to the sunglasses.

"So I picked them up and asked if I could have them, and instead of saying no, he scowled and slammed the door, which I decided to interpret as a definite yes."

Ben figured it was safe to assume Mr. Hoggenweff no longer wanted the sunglasses.

"And last but not least . . . the grand finale!" Janet sprinted through the kitchen and into the garage.

Ben didn't want to follow, but there was no way to share his tale of stinging woe without first slogging through the vast expanse of Janet's joy.

It was just lying by the side of the road!

shouted Janet from the garage.

It seemed so tragic I wanted to cry.

Ben's brain filled with grim possibilities. Had Janet brought home a dead squirrel?

But then I was inspired. You know how much I like a hard-luck case.

Ben's hopes rose a little. Perhaps the squirrel was still alive but in need of medical attention.

I said to myself, *Janet, this is nothing a little coconut oil and a few rolls of duct tape can't fix.*

Ben considered running away. But he was just too curious.

Eventually, he reached the door and he peered into the garage. There was Janet, standing proudly beside the rusted monstrosity of a tandem bicycle.

The handlebars were bent.

The seats were ripped.

The chain was stuck in place like an intricate fossil.

"There was a sign that said

FREE TO A GOOD Home!

Can you think of a better home than me, Ben?"

Ben couldn't. Janet really was the best. But it was ridiculous to think the bike would ever do more than injure careless children.

"But it's . . . junk!"

"I can see why you'd say that," said Janet, unfazed by Ben's assessment. "But *look*! This pedal still wiggles a little. I think there's hope. I see bright days ahead for you and me and Jalopy."

"Jalopy?"

"You have to agree it's the perfect name for this bike."

It definitely was. But Ben wasn't feeling agreeable.

"I owe you an apology," said Janet. "I have to admit, your fortune actually works."

"What are you talking about?" Ben was suspicious. Janet never changed her mind about anything. It was one of the most admirable and frustrating things about her.

Think about it. Coatzilla and my sunglasses and Jalopy are the *best*.

The best things in life are free.

And they were all *free*.

I dunno, Ben, maybe you're onto something.

Ben's suspicion transformed into plain old fury as the pieces clicked neatly into place. He pointed his finger and glared at Janet like a popped balloon glares at a pin. "Flegg's not the one who stole my fortune. You are!"

CHAPTER 8

"What do you mean, I stole your fortune?" Janet had the stunned expression of someone who just jumped off the high dive only to realize the pool is full of snakes. "Explain yourself, Ben."

"Before I could use the fortune to get my scooter, *you* used it to get that hideous coat!" Ben glared at Janet like a hunting dog glares at a thicket full of ducks.

Janet gasped.

Coatzilla is *beautiful*!

But Ben didn't want to hear it. He clenched
his jaw and trembled like an earthquake.

You knew how much I
wanted the Astrostar. You
knew it was my fortune.
And you used it anyway!

Janet raised her hands
in apology and surrender.

Okay, Ben, I can see you're upset. I'm
sure we can figure out how to make
everything all right again, but first tell
me exactly what happened.

Ben surprised himself by calming down.
He desperately wanted everything to be all
right again. He told Janet about the laughing
clerk and the Mega Mega. He told her all
the details that mattered and a few that
probably didn't.

Got it,

said Janet when Ben was finished.

Let's think this through. The fortune didn't work for *Flegg* because it actually belongs to *you*, right?

Ben nodded. That made sense.

And . . . let's just assume the fortune didn't work for *you* because Flegg still has the fortune itself.

You said the piece of paper didn't matter,

Ben objected.

We must consider all possibilities. Even *I* am occasionally wrong.

Ben peered at Janet with suspicion, suddenly worried she'd been brainwashed or replaced by a Janet-shaped cyborg.

68

"But most important, as you yourself already said, the things *I* got for free are *not* the best," Janet insisted, gesturing to her sunglasses and tugging the sleeve of the terrifying coat.

"Which means there's no way *I* stole your fortune. Can we agree on that, at least?"

Ben thought about it. Whether or not Janet actually believed it, Coatzilla was not the best. And the sunglasses were quite possibly the worst. She had gotten those things because no one else wanted them.

Which meant she *hadn't* stolen his fortune.

Ben removed betrayal from the list of things he felt, but devastation and despair remained.

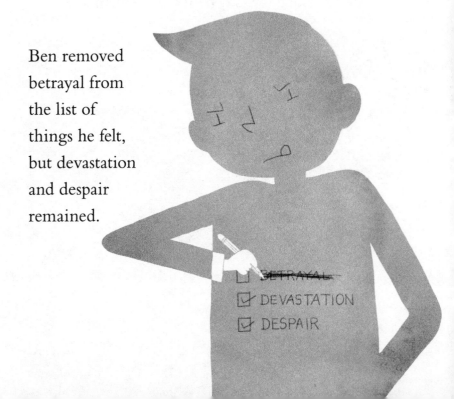

"That makes sense," Ben admitted. "But it doesn't matter now. All hope is lost."

Janet grabbed Ben's arm and gave him a fierce look. "Bite your tongue, Ben! I have a plan."

"Tell me!" Ben insisted. Janet's plans were usually good, and sometimes even great.

"Flegg has your fortune, but it doesn't work for *him,* right?"

"Right."

"But . . . if he gives it back, it should work for *you* . . . since it was yours to begin with. Does that make sense?"

Ben nodded. So far, he liked the plan a lot.

Once it starts working again, you can get your Astrostar *and* you can use it to get Flegg a bunch of free desserts. Then he won't have any reason to take *your* cookies because he'll already have as many as he wants. It's a win-win situation.

Ben was so stunned he forgot how to speak. But then he remembered.

Janet, you're a genius!

I won't deny it,

said Janet, smiling and taking an exaggerated bow.

And here's the best part. If you hadn't lost your fortune in the first place, you never would've had a chance to fix the Flegg situation.

So maybe losing my fortune was actually a *good* thing that will lead to an even better thing?

"I think so," said Janet, beaming. But then her expression fell. "As long as . . . well, you know."

"What?" Ben *didn't* know, but he wanted to.

"As long as the fortune actually . . . *works* the way you think it does." Janet had the careful expression of someone who's trying to explain to a unicorn that it's probably imaginary.

Of *course* it does,

said Ben.

And if it *doesn't* . . . ?

asked Janet gently.

It definitely *does,*

said Ben, who really wanted Janet to be on his side.

CHAPTER 9

Ben had just gotten home when his mom rushed in with a bag full of something and a face unfolding with excited expressions.

I've figured it out, she announced.

Dumbles doesn't need to go on a diet.

The vet kept saying their dog, Dumbles, was too fat and needed to stop eating table scraps. But Ben's mom found it impossible to follow that advice. Whenever Dumbles walked into the room, he'd give her a look that said, *Hey, lady. Give me some food. Or else you'll get no cuddles and licks.* And she would crumble like a sugar cube.

Ben's mom walked over to where Dumbles was happily sleeping. "How's my little Tumbly Dumbly Doo?" she said in the ridiculous voice she only used when chatting with Dumbles. "Look what I got for my *hefty-wefty boy.*"

She reached into the bag and pulled out a colorful jumble of levers and knobs. "He just needs some exercise. When he was a puppy, he ran around a lot. He just forgot how."

Ben remembered standing on the couch to keep from getting knocked over as puppy Dumbles raced around the room like a full balloon that someone let go of before tying the knot.

"The Poochinator unlocks the puppy within," Ben's mom announced, pointing to the instruction manual. "Apparently, it's foolproof!"

"Great." Ben looked over at Dumbles sound asleep in the afternoon sunlight and decided there had never been a less unlocked puppy since dogs were first invented.

His mom put the Poochinator on the floor next to Dumbles and pushed a button on a paw-shaped remote control.

A robotic *woof woof woof* echoed through the tiny speakers, and a row of multicolored lights blinked to life as a yellow bone spun inside a clear plastic dome.

Dumbles opened one eye and glanced at the Poochinator. His nostrils flared and his whiskers twitched, but every other part of him was as still as a stone.

"Look!" Ben's mom announced. "He likes it! Next we *reward* him with . . . *this*." She pressed a button, and the barking was replaced by a robotic voice that said:

"This is great," said Ben's mom, trying so hard to believe her own lie. "Run around, Dumby. Frisk and frolic those chub-chubbertons away!"

Dumbles made the dog version of a frown, then
rolled onto his back with an exasperated
sigh and placed his paw across his
obviously offended eyes.

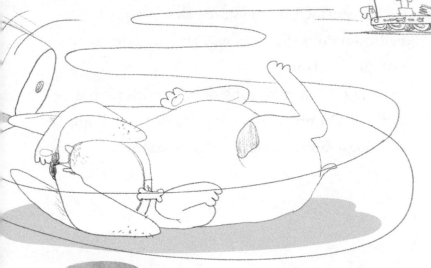

Wait. . . .

Ben's mom scanned the instructions in
search of an explanation.

FOOLPROOF!

she insisted, pointing
at the word as if Ben
were the one who had written it.

Dumbles is no fool, he thought.

Ben's mom crumpled the instructions and threw them behind the couch. "The Poochinator was not free, Dumbles!"

She stormed up the stairs. Ben heard her bedroom door shut in a way that was almost but not quite a slam.

Ben scratched Dumbles's belly with his big toe, and Dumbles heaved the deep-bellied sigh of a dog who is already perfectly happy.

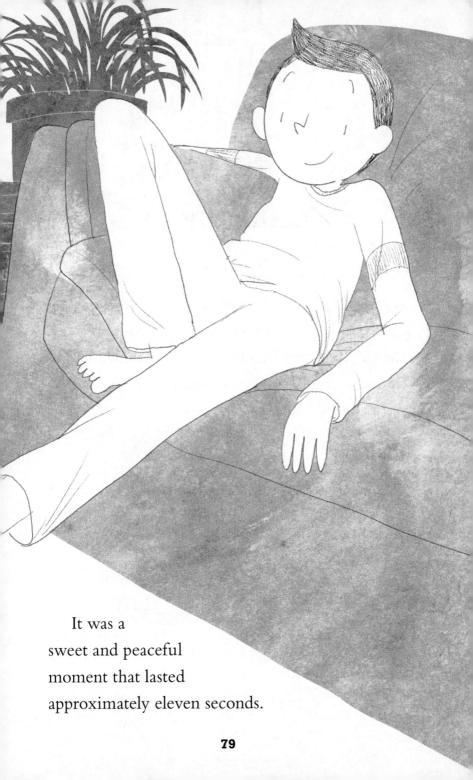

It was a
sweet and peaceful
moment that lasted
approximately eleven seconds.

CRUNCH!

CHAPTER 10

First Ben heard the awful crunching sound and wondered what it was. Next he saw the guilty look on his dad's face when he walked in from the garage. Then Ben noticed the mangled mess that used to be a scooter dangling from his dad's outstretched hands.

I *might* have hit your scooter with my car,

said Ben's dad with the worried smile he often used when Ben's mom burned the pancakes.

It *might* be time to get a new one.

Ben's ears perked up, and so did his heart. Maybe there was *another* road that led to the Astrostar!

"I'm not sure about that," said Ben's mom, bounding down the stairs in her fuzzy green evening pants, and armed with a fresh set of opinions. She was the sort of person who didn't believe in getting a new toothbrush until every last bristle was gone.

"What do you mean?" Ben wondered if they were looking at the same scooter.

She examined the tragic remains with the eye of a doctor determined to save someone's life.

I think we might be able to fix it.

The scooter responded by falling into several more pieces.

"Or maybe you're right," she admitted.

Ben's heart leapfrogged from hopeful to ecstatic.

"You can use your birthday money from Aunt Mindy," his dad suggested.

Ben's heart shriveled like grapes in the hot desert sun.

"I still can't believe she gave him so much," his mom complained. "Ben isn't ready to manage that much money."

"I had a great talk with Ben about the importance of *saving* your money," Ben's dad replied. "He really took it to heart."

Ben *sort of* remembered a conversation like that.

So now you can use it to buy a new scooter, right, Ben?

Right,

said Ben, nodding as if nodding had the power to turn back time.

"I'm proud of you," said Ben's dad, kissing Ben on the head, which he secretly loved but felt like he didn't deserve.

"All right," said Ben's mom. "I guess we should be grateful to Mindy for being so generous. We certainly can't afford a new scooter at the moment."

"*And . . . ?*" said Ben's dad to his mom, like a person throwing a baseball nice and slow for a little kid to hit. "Don't you have something to say to Ben?"

"*And . . .* and I guess I owe Ben an *apology* for doubting him," she said with the smile of someone who hates being wrong but knows she sometimes is.

I can't wait to see your new scooter, Benny.

Her hands were covered in hamburger gunk, so she gave him an elbow hug and a look of total trust that felt to Ben like a ticking time bomb.

83

CHAPTER 11

After breakfast the next morning, Ben set out on foot. It was undignified to walk to school. He found himself missing his *thump*ing scuffed scooter.

Janet wasn't there when Ben got to the corner, but he knew she was getting close. He heard the horrible scrape of metal on metal and the raspy rattle of ill-fitting parts, then the triumphant whoop of Janet defying the laws of safety and good taste.

A moment later, she coasted into view on the front seat of Jalopy, engulfed in Coatzilla and the abominable sunglasses.

Good news, Ben,

Janet sang.

She's seaworthy! There's nothing a ratchet set and a boatload of hope can't accomplish.

Hypnotized by the sheer awfulness of Jalopy, Ben hopped on. Pedaling the bike was like trying to saw through a knotty tree branch, but somehow they managed to coax the shuddering ruckus down one improbable block after another.

When they got to school and rolled up to the bike rack, the grinding clamor of Jalopy caused every head to turn. Including Flegg's.

"There he is," said Janet.

There he was. The sight of his towering foe turned Ben's steely nerves into oatmeal.

Janet gave Ben a hearty slap on the back. "Just walk right up to him, and the plan will take care of itself."

Remind me.

Ben's heart was pounding.
His brain wasn't working.

What was the plan, again?

85

Janet grabbed Ben by both shoulders and looked him in the eye.

You can do this, Ben. Flegg is a reasonable guy.

But Ben wasn't sure about that. Flegg was currently helping himself to Teddy Hornik's granola bar.

Ben was panicky and petrified. "I can't."

"Why not?"

"He's twenty times meaner and four hundred percent stronger than me."

"I get it, Ben. The numbers don't lie, but do you want that fortune back or not? Do you want Flegg to leave you alone or don't you?"

"Of course I do. But I need . . . *something.*"
Ben didn't know what kind of something it was.

"I'm right here," said Janet, encouragingly.

"I need something . . . *else*." Ben appreciated Janet, but to survive his conversation with Flegg, he needed more than she could offer.

"First of all, *ouch*." Janet was glancing around nervously like a criminal does before grabbing the loot and running for the hills. "Second, maybe you should open your—"

"Great idea!" Ben suddenly realized what Janet was going to say. He'd been so focused on the fortune he'd *lost* that he'd forgotten about the new one in his lunch. Maybe *today's* cookie contained the wisdom he needed to survive the coming hurricane.

Of course it did. Everything was going to be okay. Ben sat down, opened his lunch bag, pulled out his cookie, and—

"Ben." Janet's voice was not calm.

He lifted his eyes just a little. On the ground in front of him was a much bigger pair of sneakers than belonged on the feet of an elementary school student.

Ben didn't have the heart to look all the way up, so he looked halfway. What he saw was an outstretched palm the size of a pizza paddle.

"Cookie," said Flegg.

Ben's tongue turned to pudding. His bones disappeared. He was as helpless as a jellyfish at the bottom of a ladder.

The plan,

Janet hissed.

Remember the plan.

Ben *remembered* the plan, but his lips refused to make words.

SIGH!

"Cookie," said Flegg again, wiggling his
fingers expectantly.

Come on, Flegg,

said Janet, squeezing
herself into the extremely
small space between
Flegg and Ben.

That's not even a sentence.

Gimme cookie.

That was better,

Janet admitted.

But still rude!

Flegg's words sounded less like a request and more like a sledgehammer. With surprising agility, he reached around Janet, plucked the cookie from Ben's hand, and started to pull off the wrapper.

"That's not how it *works,* Flegg! You have to wait for the other person to actually *give* it to you," Janet insisted.

"Nope."

Ben watched with horror as Flegg popped the cookie into his mouth and started to chew.

WAIT!

Ben shrieked in a voice so shrill that Flegg looked up in surprise.

What are you *doing?*

Ea-ding duh cuh-kie,

Flegg explained without really opening his mouth.

"But . . . you didn't take the fortune out first!"

Flegg's eyebrows betrayed the slightest wiggle of surprise, but it was too late. He took a few final chews and then swallowed with deep satisfaction.

"I don't need a new fortune," he declared. "The old one is already perfect."

"But yesterday's fortune still belongs to Ben! Which is why it doesn't work for you," Janet explained, trying to salvage the smoldering wreckage of the plan. "If you'll just give it back, Ben will—"

I don't know what you're talking about,

Flegg interrupted with a menacing grin.

My fortune is working great. That was the best cookie I've ever had.

And I got it for free.

CHAPTER 12

Flegg turned and Flegged his way across the schoolyard, scattering crowds as he went.

Ben crumpled back on the bench. "I tried."

"I know," said Janet, crumpling next to him. "I did, too. Flegg is . . ."

"Flegg," said Ben. There was no other way to finish the sentence. "I'm cursed."

"You really are," Janet agreed. "But look on the bright side. You'll get a new cookie tomorrow. Maybe you should eat it for breakfast."

Ben liked the idea of cookies for breakfast.

But he didn't want another fortune. He wanted the one Flegg had stolen.

Chin up, Ben,

said a voice he didn't recognize.

Help is on the way.

Ben looked up and locked eyes with a fourth grader named Rainey Barlow, who was rolling up in her wheelchair. He didn't know her well, but he certainly knew *of* her.

Ben was honored and surprised that she seemed to be talking to *him*.

"I saw what happened to you," said Rainey with a grave expression. "I saw it yesterday, too."

Rainey looked more than just concerned. She seemed upset, like something bad had happened to *her*.

"Did Flegg take *your* cookies, too?" Ben asked.

"He might as well have. When Flegg takes cookies from *one* of us, he takes them from *all* of us, if you know what I mean."

Ben didn't know what she meant, but he liked how it sounded.

I'm here to help you get

JUSTICE.

Ben's ears perked up. Help from Rainey Barlow was an unlikely development in the war against Flegg, but he was willing to consider any possibility.

"Ben has all the help he needs," said Janet, sounding a little protective.

Rainey looked at Janet with admiration. "It was impressive how you stood up to Flegg. You're a champ in my book. But it's going to take more than one act of courage to get Ben's fortune back. We have to consider . . . *alternative solutions*."

"What does *that* mean?" asked Ben. Rainey's mysterious words were both exciting and worrisome.

Rainey glanced around as if they were being watched.

No more questions. Not here. Not now,

she said dramatically as she pulled something out of her backpack and thrust it into Ben's hands.

Give this to Preston at recess. He'll know what to do.

"Who?" asked Janet.

"Sorry. I meant to say PJ. PJ Astley. Give it to him."

With that, Rainey spun around and wheeled herself across the schoolyard. A moment later, she was situated among the other members of the Four Square Club, who gathered each morning by the flagpole.

What did she give you?

asked Janet.

Ben looked down. In his hand was a small green card that read

JUSTICE FOR ALL

Ben liked the sound of that.
Justice for *all* meant justice for *him*.

CHAPTER 13

Ben didn't know much about Rainey Barlow, but he knew a lot about Preston Astley Jr., or "PJ," as most people called him.

PJ was student council president and had been since second grade, which meant he read the morning announcements every Monday. He always won at least one category in the end-of-year talent show. He wore a shirt and tie every single day. And he was in the Four Square Club. Ben assumed he was their leader, because he always stood in the first square. PJ was usually in charge of whatever group he was in.

PRESTON ASTLEY JR.

"Wow," said Janet. She was holding the card and staring at the words.

"PJ plays four square at recess every day," said Ben.

"I've noticed," said Janet. "One time, I asked if I could play, but PJ wouldn't let me."

"Why not?"

"He said the club was just for older kids."

"That doesn't seem fair."

"That's what I said! He told me I could start my own club if I wanted to."

Principal Hogan had recently encouraged the students to start recess clubs in order to CULTIVATE OPPORTUNITIES for LEADERSHIP and CIVIC ENGAGEMENT.

Ben remembered the phrase. He liked how official it sounded.

And so there were a lot of new clubs lately:

Ben had tried a few. But none were as fun as playing kickball.

Janet was full of thoughts.

It's weird. There's a main group of kids who always show up at Four Square Club:

Rainey, PJ, PJ's best friend, Fizz, and a bunch of PJ's other friends.

And every day there's a few *different* kids, too. But it's never the *same* different kids two days in a row.

Like you have to be invited?

Exactly. And it looks like *you* just got invited.

I wonder why.

I guess we're going to find out.

You're coming with me?

Ben was relieved.

You couldn't stop me if you tried.

Ben had no intention of trying.

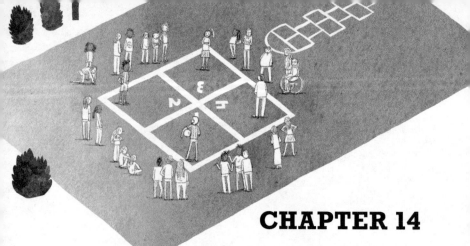

CHAPTER 14

When recess started, Ben and Janet headed over to the four square court.

PJ was standing in the first square, Fizz was in the second, and a fifth grader named Molly was in the third. In the fourth square was a fourth grader named Pamela.

The other members of the Four Square Club were gathered in a circle around the court, waiting for their turn to play.

It was the first time Ben had gotten a look at them up close. Janet was right. It was a bunch of PJ's friends, most of them fifth graders and some of the most popular kids in the school.

Rainey didn't match the rest of the group. People liked her, but she wasn't in the PJ Astley crowd.

Ben kept watching. PJ and the other players were bouncing the ball back and forth, but in a half-hearted sort of way, like no one really cared about winning.

They appeared to be deep in conversation, but instead of laughing and joking, they were serious and solemn. Ben kept waiting for someone to score a point, but it never seemed to happen.

Janet gave him a nudge. "The card."

Ben scooted forward and waved at Rainey, who noticed him and nodded in reply. The next time the ball bounced toward Molly's square, Rainey rolled over and caught it herself.

What are you doing? asked PJ impatiently.

We have visitors, said Rainey, pointing at Ben.

PJ turned and looked at Ben with irritation. "What do you want?"

Um. Ben held up the card.

I'm supposed to give this to you?

PJ blew a whistle that was hanging around his neck.

"I need a moment," he said to the other players. And then he walked over and took the card from Ben.

"Where did you get this?"

"*I* gave it to him," Rainey declared as she wheeled herself over to where they were standing. "Ben has been the victim of a grave injustice."

Now PJ seemed interested.

Go on.

Suddenly Ben got nervous. He didn't know if it was okay to look PJ in the eye. Or whether to call him sir. Instead, Ben bowed at the waist like someone greeting a king.

"It's okay, Ben," said Rainey, who seemed to understand how Ben felt. "That's not necessary. You can tell Preston what happened. He's on your side."

Ben wasn't sure, but it seemed like PJ had bristled a little when Rainey called him Preston.

Someone took my cookie, said Ben.
And stole my fortune.

His *fortune* cookie fortune, Janet clarified.
And it was a *good* one.

What was it? PJ asked.

Ben told him.

"Yeah, that is a good one," PJ agreed.

"I just want to get it back," Ben explained.

"I understand. I'm pretty sure we can help."

PJ seemed strong and sure, like someone who wasn't afraid to stand up to Flegg. Ben felt grateful and relieved.

Who's *we*?

asked Janet, eager for some answers.

"The members of
Kid Court, of course,"
said PJ with surprise.

And then his eyes
narrowed, and he looked
down at Ben and Janet like
a picnicker looks at an ant.

Wait a second.

What grade are you guys in?

Rainey's face grew panicked,
and Ben got even more confused.

Third,

Ben answered.

"Rainey!" PJ was irritated now. "You know
the rules!"

"I know!" said Rainey, wilting a little.
"But . . . some rules are meant to be broken?"

"Not this one!" PJ snapped.

"What's Kid Court?" asked Janet.

We're the keepers of justice, upholding the Code of the Schoolyard! said Rainey in an excited whisper.

I'm one of the lawyers, PJ is the judge, and they're the jury, she continued, gesturing over to the circle of kids standing around the four square court.

JURY →

JUDGE

"Why are you whispering?" Janet demanded.

"Kid Court is only for people with the *maturity* and *judgment* to keep our proceedings *top-secret,*" said PJ, glaring at Rainey as he did. "Which means fourth grade and up, no exceptions."

Janet was offended. "I'm extremely mature and judgmental!"

From the scowl on PJ's face, Ben could tell he wasn't interested in Janet's soaring opinion of her own magnificence.

"There's a good reason to make an exception, I swear," Rainey pleaded. "Tell Preston *who's* been taking your cookies."

Ben hesitated. It felt like snitching on Flegg, and it made him afraid. He didn't even want to say the name out loud.

But PJ was staring at him. *Waiting.*

Ben made up his mind and just said it. "Flegg McEggers."

PJ flinched when he heard Flegg's name. Now he was interested and maybe a little bit worried.

Fizz walked over. He'd clearly been listening.

This could be our big chance, Peej. No one's been willing to bring a case against Flegg.

"Our motto is 'Justice for *All*,' Preston," Rainey added. "Ben needs our help."

"If we take this case, who's going to be Ben's lawyer?" PJ demanded. "Who's going to have the guts to go up against Flegg?"

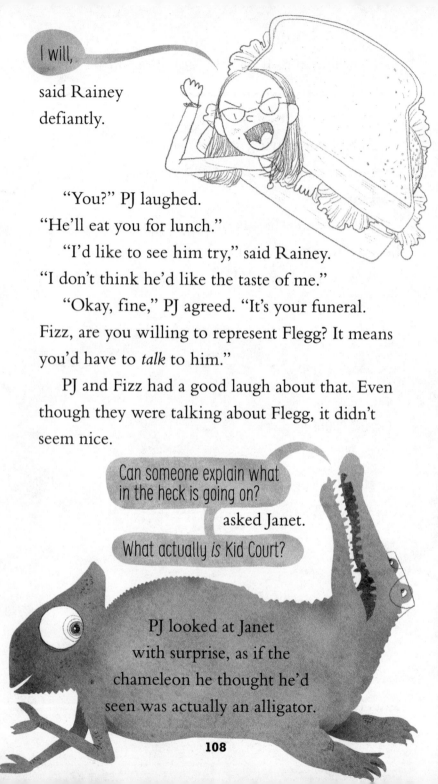

I will,

said Rainey
defiantly.

"You?" PJ laughed.
"He'll eat you for lunch."

"I'd like to see him try," said Rainey.
"I don't think he'd like the taste of me."

"Okay, fine," PJ agreed. "It's your funeral.
Fizz, are you willing to represent Flegg? It means
you'd have to *talk* to him."

PJ and Fizz had a good laugh about that. Even
though they were talking about Flegg, it didn't
seem nice.

Can someone explain what
in the heck is going on?

asked Janet.

What actually *is* Kid Court?

PJ looked at Janet
with surprise, as if the
chameleon he thought he'd
seen was actually an alligator.

"Have you had Mr. P.'s unit on the branches of government?" asked Rainey.

"We're doing it now," Ben replied.

"Great. So . . . think of the school as a smaller version of the country. Principal Hogan is the *executive* branch, like the president. He makes the big decisions, like when to have assemblies and what we eat for lunch."

Ben nodded. It made sense so far.

"But according to the Constitution, the power shouldn't all be in one person's hands," PJ added. "You need a separate *judicial* branch to make sure people follow the rules. That's Kid Court. That's us."

"Who *makes* the rules in this analogy?" asked Janet.

"The school board, I guess," said Fizz. "They're like the *legislative* branch."

"But . . . isn't Principal Hogan supposed to decide what happens when kids mess up?" asked Ben. As much as he liked the *sound* of Kid Court, it didn't seem like something that would actually work. They were just kids, after all.

"The *Sixth Amendment* to the **Constitution** says you're supposed to be judged by a jury of your *peers,*" Rainey explained. "Principal Hogan is a nice guy, don't get me wrong. But he doesn't understand what we go through. He hasn't been a kid for a long time."

That made sense to Ben, too. Being a kid was so different from being an adult.

"If you get sent to Principal Hogan, he'll give you detention or make you stack chairs during recess. Or . . . worst of all . . . give you a *strike*."

When the word "strike" came tumbling out of Rainey's mouth, everyone shuddered a little.

Ben knew what happened when you got three strikes. Your parents came. And then they took you away. And you didn't come back for a few days, or sometimes even longer.

"We think most problems can be solved *without* anyone getting a strike," said Rainey.

That sounded good to Ben, too. But maybe a little too good to be true. "Even Flegg problems?"

"Even *Flegg* problems," Rainey insisted.

I founded Kid Court to provide justice for all,

said PJ, who was clearly proud of himself.

Cofounded,

said Rainey delicately, looking at PJ the way a ladder looks at the person who's standing on it.

Cofounded,

PJ echoed, as if the word tasted sour.

In any case, I'm chief justice of Kid Court. I'm also president of student council. And president and founder of Four Square Club.

It was like PJ was trying to prove something, which seemed strange, since he was already the one in charge.

"*Co*founder of Four Square Club," said Rainey, even more delicately.

But this time PJ ignored her completely.

So . . . you'll help me?

asked Ben.

PJ looked at Ben like a scale looks at the person it's trying to weigh.

"Come on, Peej," Fizz pleaded. "This might be our best chance to stop Flegg."

"All right," said PJ, shaking his head. "We'll make an exception just this once."

"Thanks," said Ben.

"But keep your mouth shut about Kid Court," said PJ, glaring down at Ben and Janet. "And don't come crying to me if this doesn't work. Going up against Flegg is a dangerous game. We can't protect you from him."

Don't worry, said Janet.

I can.

Ben knew Janet believed what she was saying. He just wasn't sure he believed it himself.

"Are you in?" asked PJ impatiently.

"We can do this, Ben," Rainey insisted.

Ben hesitated. When the day began, all he'd wanted was his Astrostar, but the stakes seemed so much higher now.

"How about this," said PJ. "We have a trial to finish. Why don't you watch and see how it works? And *then* you can decide."

Ben nodded. If he had to make a decision, later was certainly better than now.

CHAPTER 15

As PJ and the other players went back to the four square court, Rainey joined Ben and Janet.

"I'm confused," Janet admitted. "Is this a Kid Court trial or a four square game?"

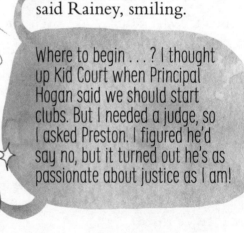

Both,

said Rainey, smiling.

Where to begin . . . ? I thought up Kid Court when Principal Hogan said we should start clubs. But I needed a judge, so I asked Preston. I figured he'd say no, but it turned out he's as passionate about justice as I am!

Rainey's eyes were full of stars.

asked Janet. There was no kingdom she didn't want to rule.

"I'd love to be a judge . . . *someday*," Rainey replied. "But the chief justice of Kid Court has to command the respect of the entire school, and PJ is so . . ."

"So . . . *what?*" Janet folded her arms and squinted.

"You know . . . he's super smart and has lots of friends, which is helpful, since we also needed a jury. I track down new cases, and PJ runs the trials. We make the perfect team."

"What does all that have to do with four square?" Janet prompted, rolling her eyes a little.

"Right," said Rainey. "When Preston proposed Kid Court, Principal Hogan said justice was *his* job, and if he caught us doing trials in the schoolyard, he'd make us scrape the gum pole."

"Yikes," said Janet.

"Exactly," said Rainey. "We needed to figure out how to have a trial while making it look like we *weren't* having a trial, so I came up with Four Square Club, which is actually just Kid Court in disguise."

"That sounds very complicated," said Ben.

"Justice often is."

"If Kid Court is so top-secret, why are you breaking the rules for Ben?" asked Janet skeptically.

"Because someone has to put a stop to Flegg, and Preston knows it," Rainey fired back. "Flegg's been awful to him, too. And to Fizz. And to most of the kids on the jury."

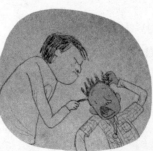

"Did he do something to *you*?" Ben asked. He wanted to understand why she cared so much.

"Flegg's been awful to *all* of us," said Rainey, "which is why *all* of us should know about Kid Court. Next year, after PJ goes off to Honeycutt Academy, maybe we'll open it up to younger kids, too."

"He's going to the academy?" Janet asked.

HONEYCUTT ACADEMY

was the private school in town. Some kids went there instead of the public middle school. It was really hard to get into. "He's applying," said Rainey, "but he'll get in for sure. Did you know they have the number-one-ranked debate team in the state? It's the *perfect* place for Preston. He's bound for *greatness*."

Janet rolled her eyes at Ben, but Rainey didn't see. "Aren't we supposed to be watching the trial?" she prompted.

PLAINTIFF

"Right," said Rainey, turning back to the game. "Let me catch you up. Pamela is the *plaintiff*." Rainey pointed as she explained. "That means she's the one who got mad and asked for the trial. If it helps you remember, 'plaintiff' sort of sounds like 'complain.' The *plaintiff* is the one who *complains* that they've been mistreated, got it?"

Ben nodded. He liked learning new words.

"David is the *defendant*. He's the one who Pamela says did something wrong, so now he has to *defend* himself."

"What did he do?" Ben was excited. It was kind of like watching a movie starring people he knew.

118

"There was a substitute teacher in fourth grade last Friday. It was Pamela's turn to read morning announcements, but David convinced the sub it was *his* turn, so *he* read them instead and got the Honeycutt Elementary pencil that was supposed to be Pamela's prize."

"Rude!" said Janet.

"Agreed," Rainey replied. "But Fizz pointed out that in third grade, Pamela did the same thing to David and got the Honeycutt refrigerator magnet that should have been *his,* so now things are even-steven."

"Oh," said Janet. "That changes everything."

"Right?" said Rainey. "Isn't justice *interesting*?"

But also complicated, Ben thought. The trial had made sense when there was a good guy and a bad guy. Now there were two bad guys. Or was it two good guys? He wasn't sure.

"All of that was covered in the opening statements by Molly and Fizz, who are the lawyers for this case," Rainey explained. "Which happened before you guys showed up. Now it's time for witness testimony."

"What's that?" asked Ben.

"The people who saw the crime occur are the witnesses. Molly will try to make David's witnesses seem like they can't be trusted, and Fizz is going to try to do the same to Pamela's."

"Why?" It sounded like a lot of work to Ben.

"It's all about convincing the jury," Rainey explained, pointing to the group of kids standing around the court. "They decide who wins the trial. Which is why you need to have a good lawyer."

Are you a good lawyer?

asked Ben. He wasn't trying to be rude, but the answer felt important.

I am,

replied Rainey with a confident smile that made Ben feel confident himself.

"Here's the first witness," she announced as a girl named Lizzie stepped into the fourth square.

Ben listened as Lizzie and then two other girls claimed David was guilty, and three boys said he was innocent. As each witness took their turn, they stepped into the fourth square and bounced the ball back and forth while answering questions from Molly and Fizz.

By the time it was done, Ben had no idea who to believe or who to trust. He was glad it wasn't his job to figure out who was right and who was wrong.

The kids in the jury gathered in a clump and had a conversation Ben couldn't hear. They didn't talk long before coming back and handing PJ a piece of paper, from which he read out loud.

In the case before us today, the jury finds the defendant GUILTY AS CHARGED!

Pamela cheered, and David slumped.

"However," PJ continued, "the jury notes that David only took Pamela's pencil after she took his magnet. I hereby sentence David to giving Pamela his pencil, and Pamela to giving David her magnet."

"The magnet fell off the fridge, and my dog chewed it up," Pamela explained.

"I was afraid of something like that," said PJ with a grave expression. "In that case, David has to give Pamela the pencil, but he gets to take her next two turns reading morning announcements."

I guess I can live with that, said Pamela.

Yeah, that seems fair, said David.

I call this session of Kid Court to a close, said PJ.

Justice has been served! said Rainey, giddy with excitement.

That was a very reasonable solution, Janet agreed.

David and Pamela went off to find their friends, and the members of the jury started playing *actual* four square.

PJ walked over to Ben. "So, are you interested?"

"Yes!" Ben replied.

The jury would find Flegg guilty.

PJ would make him return Ben's fortune.

And that

would be that.

"Okay," said PJ. "Rainey, make sure Ben's case is eligible."

"*Eligible?*" asked Janet as PJ and Fizz headed back to the four square court.

"Ben needs to find at least three witnesses willing to back up his story," Rainey explained. "It's how we make sure only solid cases come to Kid Court."

"No problem," said Janet. "Ben already has me. Plus, pretty much *everyone* saw what happened. Getting two more witnesses will be easy."

"We'll see," said Rainey, who didn't sound convinced. "I hope you're right."

"I always am," said Janet.

It wasn't *quite* true. Janet was *almost* always right, but every once in a while, her legendary confidence bonked its head on the low-hanging ceiling of reality.

Ben crossed his fingers and hoped this wasn't one of those times.

CHAPTER 16

By the time he got back to class, Ben was feeling confident. He had lots of friends, including Kyle and Lang, who he ate lunch with every single day. They read the same books. They went to each other's birthday parties. They'd known each other since kindergarten. Kyle and Lang would be his other two witnesses.

When lunchtime came, Ben sat down at the table and dived right in.

I'm not sure you guys saw, but Flegg took my cookie again today.

I saw,

said Kyle.

Everyone did,

said Lang.

I bet it was embarrassing.

"It *was*," Ben agreed. "But there's a way for you guys to help."

"What is it?" asked Kyle suspiciously.

What if there was a *top-secret organization* that could stop Flegg from ever bothering me again?

Ben tried to make it sound exciting.

There's a *top-secret organization*?

Lang whispered with wide eyes.

"Yes, but . . . you guys can't say *anything*."

"We never would," Lang promised.

"What do we have to do?" asked Kyle, who seemed willing to listen.

"Say you saw Flegg steal my cookie."

"No problem," said Lang. "I can do that."

"Say it to *who*?" Kyle was suspicious again.

"I can't tell you yet," Ben explained. "Top-secret, remember?"

"Would Flegg find out?" asked Lang.

Kyle and Lang looked at Ben like two planes wanting to land but needing to know if the runway was icy.

Ben saw no choice but to tell the truth. "Yeah. He'd be standing right there."

"No way, then," said Kyle. "Flegg is scarier than Blug Glub Glub."

Blug Glub Glub was a ferocious space monster from their favorite book series, Captain A-OK. Blug Glub Glub was known for eating entire planets.

"That's true," said Ben, sensing an opportunity. "But Captain A-OK beats him eventually, right?"

"Eventually, maybe," said Kyle. "But a lot of planets get swallowed along the way."

"But the planet he's trying to swallow is me!" said Ben, hoping for a little sympathy. "And you guys can help!"

Just get in your spaceship and fly away,

said Kyle.

You're faster than he is.

Maybe it was true, but Ben was tired of constantly running.

"Don't you want to stop Flegg from taking your cupcakes?" Ben tried to put it in terms that would make sense to Lang.

"Yeah, but . . ." Lang looked sheepish. "At least I still have *one*."

Ben was getting impatient. "This is a matter of *justice,* you guys. I really need your help!"

"Sorry, Ben," said Kyle. "It's my birthday next weekend. I want to live to see it."

Ben looked at Lang with a face that said, *Please.*

"I want to live to see Kyle's birthday, too," said Lang, not quite meeting Ben's eyes.

Ben grabbed his lunch and stomped away. He wasn't hungry anymore. He was mad and confused, but one thing was certain. If he lived to see Kyle's birthday, he definitely wasn't going to the party.

CHAPTER 17

Ben was marching angrily toward the trash cans when he spotted something that gave him the tiniest glimmer of hope.

Walter and Darby were sitting at the same table. They were bent over a single piece of paper and seemed to be having an intense conversation.

Walter was Ben's oldest friend, and Darby was his newest one. Ben felt bad asking for their help because he hadn't eaten lunch with them in a long time. But he knew he had to try.

"Can I . . . join you guys?"

Of course, said Walter with the widest smile.

Anytime. *Always.*

Sure, Ben, said Darby without looking up.

"We're working on something," Walter explained, getting louder and more excited with every passing word. "Something *big*."

"What is it?" Ben looked at the paper, which was covered in numbers and symbols.

"A statistical analysis of cafeteria food," Darby replied. "For the past three weeks, I've been tracking the occurrences of green beans, nuggets, and that orange stuff, trying to identify patterns."

The idea was unexpected, but Ben was not surprised. Darby was good at math.

"Dad has been teaching me statistics and probability. If you know what to do with numbers, you can figure out basically anything. Data is power."

Ben liked the sound of that. He needed some power. "What have you figured out so far?"

"Well, either there's someone trapped in the kitchen, sending secret codes and begging to be rescued, or Principal Hogan is trying his hardest to make us cry."

"Could it be both?"

"I'm considering every possibility."

Ben sat there for a minute, watching Darby scrawl numbers with astonishing speed.

Ben wanted to wait for the perfect moment, but lunch would soon be over. "I . . . need to ask you guys a favor."

"What is it, Ben?" asked Walter. "Do you need to borrow my sweater?"

Ben smiled. Walter was the kind of friend who would actually give you the sweater off his back if you needed it. Or one of his shoes. Or both of them.

"Nope. It's even bigger than that. And slightly dangerous. And totally *top-secret*."

Finally, Darby was intrigued enough to look up from his numbers. "What is it?"

Ben wanted to tell them, but first he had to make sure they were willing to help.

"Did you guys see Flegg take my cookie this morning?"

"I did," said Walter sadly. "And yesterday. It was awful. I wish I could have helped, but . . . you know."

"Yeah," said Ben. "I do."

"Flegg takes my snickerdoodles every day," Walter continued. "*Every* day. For a while, I tried to stop him, but he always took them anyway. So now I just hand them to him as soon as I get to school so we can skip the part where he explains all the bad things that will happen if I don't."

"Someone ought to put a stop to it." Darby seemed mad.

"Actually, I'm planning to," said Ben. "But I need your help."

"No problem, Ben," said Walter. "Tell me what to do, and I'll do it."

"All you have to do is say what you saw. . . .
But . . . you'll have to say it in front of Flegg."
Walter flinched.

Flegg once told me he'd turn me into a pancake if I ever looked at him again. I like *eating* pancakes. But I definitely don't want to *be* one.

Ben's heart fell. If Walter wasn't willing to help him, no one would.

"But as long as I don't actually have to *look* at him, I'll do it," said Walter with a toothy smile. "Do I have to look at him?"

Ben couldn't imagine there was a Kid Court rule about having to look at the defendant. "I don't think so."

"Then no problem!"

Ben's heart lifted halfway.

"How about you?" he asked Darby as delicately as he could. As it turned out, he didn't have to worry.

134

"I'm in," said Darby without hesitation. "I haven't had a cookie in a month. If you have a way to stop Flegg, sign me up."

"I think I do," said Ben, more certain with every passing second. "Are you guys sure? This could be *dangerous*."

One hundred percent, said Darby.

Of course, said Walter.

What's the worst that could happen?

A million terrible possibilities raced through Ben's brain, but he pushed them aside and decided to focus on the one *best* thing that might happen instead.

"Thanks, guys," said Ben. "I'll explain all the details as soon as I can."

He looked over at Kyle and Lang, who were laughing about something.

Ben realized he'd been eating lunch at the wrong table for a really long time.

CHAPTER 18

Lunch was about to end, so Ben glanced over to the table where the Four Square Club was eating. But Rainey wasn't there. He looked around and saw her sitting by herself at the far side of the cafeteria, surrounded by a pile of papers and notepads.

Ben walked over. "I found my three witnesses."

"Good work," said Rainey. "I'm impressed."

As Ben told her the names, she wrote them down on pieces of paper, which she handed to Ben.

What's a sub-poe-enn-ah?

he asked, stumbling his way through the puzzling word at the top of the page.

It's pronounced "suh-PEE-nuh," rhymes with "hyena,"

Rainey replied.

The *b* is silent but mighty.

"What's a—"

"A subpoena is just an order from Preston to appear in Kid Court. Hand one to each of your witnesses and say, 'You've been served.' And be sure to scowl a little."

"Why do I scowl?"

"To let them know you mean it. And to make sure they don't change their minds."

"They wouldn't! They're my friends."

Rainey patted Ben's hand like a firefighter pats a sooty puppy. "I know you believe that, but witnesses sometimes get cold feet. Once they've been handed a subpoena, they can't back out, because then they're bound by the Code of the Schoolyard to show up."

"What's the Code of—"

"Wait. . . ." Rainey grabbed Ben's arm. "You mean, you don't know?"

Ben shook his head.

"The Code of the Schoolyard is the sacred obligation of every Honeycutt student to follow the rules of fairness and justice that bind us all. Without the code, everything would fall apart. Which is why *everyone* has to follow it."

What about all the kids who don't even know about it?

Ben objected.

That's a strong point . . . ,

said Rainey,

seeming deflated.

Which is more than half the school.

"This is the problem with Preston's rules!" blurted Rainey in frustration. Then she took a deep breath and composed herself. "Maybe your case will convince him that third graders are trustworthy, too. Baby steps, right?"

"Right," said Ben.

"To review," said Rainey in a tone that was all business, "give the subpoenas to your witnesses. Remember to scowl. And meet me by the bike rack tomorrow morning ten minutes before the bell rings!"

Ben nodded and walked across the lunchroom to give Walter and Darby their subpoenas.

He gave Janet hers when they got back to Mr. P.'s classroom.

He didn't scowl, and he didn't say "You've been served," because they were his friends, and he knew they'd always have his back, no matter what.

CHAPTER 19

That night Ben's mom brought home an even bigger box. Ben followed her into the living room.

"I did some online research, and it turns out Dumbles is way too smart for the Poochinator," Ben's mom explained. "What he needs is a friend."

She opened the box and pulled out a dog–shaped robot with wheels on the bottom of its feet.

"Big Rex is the perfect pal,"

she read from the side of the box.

"He'll teach your old dog new tricks. He'll get your lazy mutt in shape."

Ben flipped a switch on the back of Big Rex's head. His robot eyes glowed creepily.

"Doesn't that sound good, Ben?" Ben's mom continued. "Rex will keep Dumbles company while we're gone during the day."

Ben glanced over at Dumbles, who didn't look like a dog who needed a friend.

Ben's mom turned a knob on the remote, and Big Rex lurched forward. She pressed a button, and Rex started looping around the room in wider and wider circles.

She was having a great time, but Dumbles didn't lift his head or even open an eye.

141

Ben's mom pressed the button again, and Big Rex raced faster, then faster still, then crashed into the bookshelf, causing a tall glass vase to fall off and shatter in a glorious tsunami of jagged fragments.

GRAB DUMBLES AND GET UP ON THE COUCH, BEN!

she shouted, breaking into what Ben liked to think of as Mom Mode.

YOU'LL CUT YOUR FEET TO SHREDS!

With considerable effort, Ben scooped
Dumbles off the floor, climbed onto the couch,
and settled in to watch as his mom swept and
vacuumed and then swept again.

Throughout the furious cleaning, Big Rex lay
on his side in the corner, his lonely eyes glowing.

Ben watched
the excitement as
Dumbles rested
gently on his lap,
completely
asleep and
perfectly
content.

CHAPTER 20

When Ben and Janet got to school the next day,
Rainey was already there.

"Good morning," she said. "It's a good day for
justice, don't you think?"

She reached into her briefcase and pulled out
a box of chocolates.

"What's this for?" asked Ben.

Rainey's eyes were full of purpose and a hint
of mischief.

We have our plaintiff. That's you.
Janet, Walter, and Darby are our
witnesses. Now we need a defendant.

You mean Flegg?

Rainey nodded. "We need to let him know you're bringing a case against him and that he'll have to come to Kid Court."

"So, we have to give him a subpoena, too?"

"Exactly." Rainey was pleased that Ben understood. "But this is where things get tricky. Your friends were just willing to *take* their subpoenas. Flegg probably won't be."

Ben had so many questions, but it seemed like Rainey was brimming with answers.

But once Flegg has his subpoena, he'll be bound by the

CODE OF THE SCHOOLYARD

and he'll *have* to come to Kid Court. And from there, it's an open-and-shut case.

Bing.

Bang.

Boom.

Ben had the impression Rainey was trying to convince herself that what she was saying was true. Like someone who was actually pretty nervous. Ben wanted Rainey to be confident.

"*Guys,*" said Janet, pointing over her shoulder. There was Flegg, making his way toward them, even more quickly than usual.

"Drat! Take this. No time to explain." Rainey shoved the box into Ben's hands and wheeled herself away.

A moment later, Flegg was there, looming over Ben like an avalanche preparing to knock down some pine trees.

Hi, Ben. Where's my *free* cookie?

"I . . . don't have any cookies today." It was a lie. Today's cookie was in his sweatshirt pocket. Ben patted it nervously just to make sure. "But I do have . . . this." Ben lifted the box of chocolates for Flegg to see.

"Are you *giving* that to me?" Flegg glared at Ben warily.

Ben looked into Flegg's eyes and saw a complicated blend of suspicion and hope. It was the expression of someone who wasn't used to getting presents.

Ben wasn't sure why Rainey had handed him the chocolates, but surely he wasn't supposed to just *give* them to Flegg. Or *was* he?

"I don't *think* so," said Ben as convincingly as he could, which wasn't very convincingly at all.

"Good," said Flegg. "I prefer taking things."

Flegg grabbed the box and pried off the lid. His cruel smile twisted into a sneer.

What's this?

Flegg lifted a piece of paper from the box and peered at it.

"That is a subpoena to appear in Kid Court," said Rainey, returning triumphantly from where she'd been waiting to pounce.

You've been *served*!

It was stunning, seeing Rainey next to Flegg. It was like a strawberry trying to intimidate a watermelon.

What? said Flegg, pulling his eyes away from the subpoena and looking down at Rainey.

"Bring this to the four square court at recess," she replied, holding up a bright red card. "Unless you decide to seek your own legal counsel, an attorney will be provided for you."

"Why are you talking like that?" Flegg was annoyed.

"I'm a lawyer. That's how we talk."

"You're not a lawyer."

Rainey bristled. "For the purposes of today, I am."

"You're not," Flegg argued. "And I'm not coming to whatever this is." Flegg dropped the empty box on the ground. He crumpled the subpoena in his powerful hands.

Rainey looked stunned, like someone had just drilled a ⬤ hole in the side of her canoe.

But . . . you *have* to. By the authority of Chief Justice Preston Astley Jr. and the Code of the Schoolyard, anyone summoned to Kid Court must appear and face justice!

"I'm not afraid of PJ," said Flegg, "and I don't know what those other things are. I never agreed to them."

Rainey was irate. "The Code of the Schoolyard isn't something you *agree* to," she shouted. "It's something that just *is*!"

"Maybe for you," said Flegg. "Not for me."

He gave a final scowl, then turned and Flegged away.

For just a glimmer of a second, Ben understood how Flegg must have felt. Ben hadn't known about the Code of the Schoolyard until yesterday. And even though Flegg was in fifth grade and *should* have been in on the secret, he didn't know, either. No one ever told Flegg anything. Because everyone was always trying so hard to avoid him.

Ben looked at Janet, and Janet looked at Ben.
They both looked at Rainey, who was tapping on
her briefcase and muttering to herself.

Think, Rainey, think. What would
Preston do? What would Preston do?

We could ask him,

Janet suggested,
gesturing over to
the flagpole, where
the other members
of the Four Square
Club had gathered.

He's standing
right there.

No!

said Rainey angrily.

And then she took a deep breath and smoothed
her blazer and spoke like someone trying to be
calm. "No. I want Preston to see I can handle
this case by myself. Which I absolutely can. We
just need to try a different approach."

"I thought Kid Court *was* the different approach," Janet pointed out.

"It was *supposed* to be," Rainey admitted.

"So we need a *different* different approach?" asked Janet, one of her eyebrows slightly higher than the other.

Rainey's eyes got wide. "Janet, you're a genius!"

"I *am*?" said Janet. And then she caught herself. "I mean of *course* I am. But why are you saying it now?"

"Sometimes cases settle *out* of court. It's a perfectly respectable alternative to a trial." Rainey was excited. She drummed her fingers on top of her briefcase.

"The question is this: If Flegg won't listen to the Code of the Schoolyard, who *will* he listen to?"

"Principal Hogan?" Janet suggested.

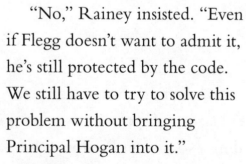

THREE STRIKES!

"No," Rainey insisted. "Even if Flegg doesn't want to admit it, he's still protected by the code. We still have to try to solve this problem without bringing Principal Hogan into it."

"Who else will Flegg listen to?" asked Ben.

"Exactly!" said Rainey. "I have research to do. And materials to prepare. There isn't much time."

Ben could see her brain gnawing on a question. He wished he could peek inside and see the answer.

Rainey broke out of her daze for just a moment, as if suddenly realizing Ben and Janet were still there. "Gotta go. Meet me by the trophy case at recess."

And with that, she raced off like a house cat determined to prove it's actually a tiger.

CHAPTER 21

Instead of rushing out to the schoolyard when recess came, Ben and Janet turned the other way and headed to the lobby. Rainey was waiting by the trophy case, beaming as if she'd just opened a fresh can of moxie and intended to eat it for lunch.

"What's the plan?" Ben was excited. He needed to know.

Come with me. I'll tell you on the way.

Rainey blazed down the hallway, pressed the elevator button, and rolled inside. Janet followed, and so did Ben. He'd never been inside the school elevator.

It felt deliciously forbidden.

"We're going to see Ms. Mung," Rainey explained as the doors closed and the elevator started to rise. "She's on recess duty Mondays, Wednesdays, and Fridays, but on Tuesdays and Thursdays, she stays in her classroom and practices accordion."

Ms. Mung was the fifth-grade teacher. Which meant she was Flegg's teacher.

"Wait. *What?*" Janet was intrigued. "Are you a lawyer or a spy?"

"Let's just say I've been doing my homework," Rainey replied with a smile. "Ms. Mung will be my teacher next year. I have to be prepared."

When the elevator opened on the second floor, they heard a cheerful, wheezing waltz echoing down the hallway.

"She's not bad," said Janet admiringly as they followed Rainey toward the fifth-grade classroom.

"Practice makes perfect," said Rainey.

Ben couldn't argue with that.

They waited outside the classroom until the song ended, at which point Rainey knocked sharply on the door.

A moment later, it opened, and there was Ms. Mung with her hair pulled back and a shiny white accordion hanging from a red strap around her neck.

Hello . . . Rainey. What is it?

Ms. Mung seemed surprised, but her voice was kind.

You've heard of me?

Rainey was pleased.

I certainly have. What can I do for you?

We have a pressing matter to discuss. May we come in?

Of course,

said Ms. Mung with a smile.

They headed into the classroom and gathered around one of the group tables. Rainey opened her briefcase and handed Ms. Mung a piece of paper.

Do you know this person?

Is this . . . Flegg McEggers?

Ben arched his neck to see the paper, which featured a drawing of Flegg that was actually pretty good.

I'm guessing you know he's one of my students?

I do. He's also a fugitive from the law. He's stolen two of Ben's cookies and two of his fortunes.

"That's terrible," said Ms. Mung, shaking her head with an expression that was pained but not surprised. "How can I help?"

"Ben tried to get his fortune back, but Flegg wouldn't listen to reason," Rainey explained. "And we really don't want to get Principal Hogan involved. Maybe you could help?"

"It was kind of you to come to me first. I'll talk to Flegg right after recess."

"How about now?" Rainey countered. "Ben needs to get that fortune back as soon as possible."

Ben looked out the window, which had a good view of the schoolyard. There was Flegg, taking Wallace Poplar's gummy bears.

He's right outside.

Ms. Mung made a face that was sad but determined and walked over to the phone on the wall.

Mr. Butter, would you please get Flegg McEggers and ask him to come to my classroom? Thank you.

And then she turned back and looked at Ben. "I want you to know . . ." Ms. Mung clasped her hands nervously. "I'm not trying to excuse what Flegg did. It's not right that he took your cookies. But in my experience, underneath it all, he's a good person who makes consistently bad decisions."

Ben was surprised. This version of Flegg sounded nothing like the person who'd been making his life miserable for the past few days.

Then why is he such a jerk to me?

"I don't know," Ms. Mung admitted. "But however much it might feel like he's picking on you, I'm guessing it's not actually *about* you."

To Ben, it was not helpful to hear Flegg was a good guy underneath. It was complicated and confusing.

From the twisted shapes of Janet's and Rainey's eyebrows, they seemed to agree.

They all sat there awkwardly waiting.

"Maybe . . . you could play us a song?" Rainey suggested.

Ms. Mung blushed and smiled and wiggled her fingers on the accordion keys. "I'm not very good."

"We'll be the judge of that," said Rainey, smiling.

Ms. Mung played. Ben marveled as her fingers danced, doing the hard work of making a song while his ears got the pleasant task of making it a concert. It was a happy tune with a rousing beat that filled Ben's heart with light.

Just as the song reached its glorious crescendo, Flegg walked into the room in a mood that resembled a funeral march.

CHAPTER 22

"Come in, Flegg," said Ms. Mung.
"Yes, ma'am." Flegg stood quietly with
his hands folded behind his back.
Ben was surprised.
He'd never seen Flegg listen to *anyone*.
"I hear you have something that
belongs to Ben," said Ms. Mung
softly. "Is that true?"
"No, ma'am."
"So you *didn't* take Ben's fortune?"
Her voice was steady and
certain and kind.

Yes, ma'am. I did.

"Don't you think you should give it back?"

Flegg paused. He looked at Ms. Mung. Then at Ben. Then at Ms. Mung again. And then he shook his head and stared down at the floor.

Ms. Mung opened her mouth, but before she could speak, Rainey cut in.

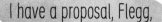

I have a proposal, Flegg,

she said, wheeling over to where he was standing.

Maybe we can settle your dispute with Ben in a way that keeps anyone from getting in trouble.

What do you mean?

Flegg seemed interested.

How about a straight-up trade? You give Ben his old fortune in exchange for the new one in his pocket.

WHAT?

Ben hadn't agreed to this!

"What makes you think I have a cookie in my pocket?" Ben demanded.

"You were fiddling with it earlier," Rainey explained. "I pay attention, Ben."

"I really want to keep this one," he pleaded.

Rainey shot Ben a look as pointed as a pin.

Do you want your fortune back or not?

"Yes, but . . ." Ben was frustrated, but Rainey was right. Getting his old fortune back was the most important thing.

Reluctantly, Ben handed his cookie to Rainey.

Flegg's eyes grew as round as moons. He reached for the cookie, but Rainey held it behind her back, just out of reach. "What do you say, Flegg? Do we have a deal?"

"Yeah," Flegg replied, "whatever you say. Let me have that cookie."

"*After* you return Ben's fortune."

But it was too late. In one astonishing motion, Flegg reached around Rainey, grabbed the cookie, pulled off the wrapper, and popped it into his mouth.

"Mmmmm," said Flegg as Ben lamented the tragic demise of yet another fortune.

"Flegg!" Ms. Mung scolded. "You agreed to trade that cookie for the fortune you already took. Please give it to Ben *immediately*!"

Flegg chewed and swallowed, and then his face settled into a mournful expression.

I would..., he said. But... I can't.

"And why is that?" Ms. Mung insisted.

"I . . . *lost* it."

"Is that true?"

Flegg nodded.

Ben was furious. He knew Flegg hadn't lost the fortune, but there was no way to prove it.

"I see," said Ms. Mung, who didn't seem convinced, either. "Do you have something to say to Ben, at least?"

"I'm sorry, Ben," said Flegg with eyes that weren't sorry. "Do you forgive me?"

Ben didn't know what to do. He was *supposed* to forgive people who apologized. But he really didn't *want* to. Flegg kept taking his cookies. Flegg made him feel scared and helpless and small. Flegg had stolen the best fortune he'd ever gotten and refused to give it back!

One fake sorry wasn't enough.

"Well, Ben?" Ms. Mung prompted. "Do you accept Flegg's apology?"

"No." Ben looked at the ground, his jaw set, his fists clenched. "I don't."

"Well, then," said Ms. Mung with a heavy sigh. "We'd better go see Principal Hogan."

Rainey's face flushed red with frustration, like she wanted to say something but knew there was nothing left to say.

She'd thrown Flegg a lifeline, and he'd cut it in two.

"But . . . I already have two strikes," said Flegg in the helpless tone of someone who's dug a hole so deep they can't get out.

"I'm sorry, Flegg," said Ms. Mung. "Please come with me."

As they walked down the hall, nobody looked at anyone else.

"But you don't understand," Flegg pleaded. "I *can't* get three strikes. My mom will be so mad. She'll yell at me. And ground me. She'll think I'm a dummy. Just give me one more chance."

Just one more chance!

Flegg didn't seem scary anymore. He just seemed scared.

"I'm sorry, Flegg," said Ms. Mung again. Ben could tell she was sad. That she wanted to help but didn't know how.

As they rode down the elevator in silence, Ben thought about Principal Hogan's three-strikes policy. If Flegg got one more, then Flegg was *out*. Which was exactly what Ben wanted. *Wasn't* it?

Weirdly, he wasn't sure.

Ben definitely wanted to get his fortune back.

Rainey wanted Flegg to go to Kid Court.

Flegg wanted to avoid Principal Hogan.

Maybe there was a way for everyone to get what they wanted.

They were almost to Principal Hogan's office. It was now or never.

"I accept," Ben blurted.

Ms. Mung stopped and looked at Ben with a puzzled expression. "What do you mean?"

"I accept Flegg's apology."

"Really?" said Flegg, his eyes wide and hopeful but still not quite ready to believe his ears.

Really?

asked Rainey.

Yes,

said Ben, nodding.

But there's a catch.

Flegg's mistrustful look returned.

What is it?

I want you to come play four square at recess tomorrow. To prove everything is cool between us.

Rainey's face lit up as Flegg's fell, like a streetlight coming on when the sun goes down.

Ms. Mung looked pleased. And relieved. "That's very generous of you, Ben. Does this seem like a good solution, Flegg?"

Flegg looked like a fox that just noticed the brand-new barbed wire fence around the chicken coop.

Yeah,

he said, staring at Ben with an unsettling combination of gratitude and rage.

"Well, good. I'm glad that's settled," said Ms. Mung. "Why don't you all head back outside to catch the end of recess?"

"Great," said Rainey. "Thank you," she called as Ms. Mung walked back down the hall.

Rainey was ecstatic. She reached into the pocket of her blazer and pulled out the red card.

Here, she said, handing it to Flegg.

You're going to need this. Recess. Tomorrow. Four square court. *Be there.*

Flegg glared at them and seethed.

I'll play your stupid game. But it's not going to change anything.

"Kid Court is not stupid!" Rainey insisted. "And it definitely isn't a game."

"Whatever," said Flegg. He took the card and shoved it into his pocket. And then he stormed off down the hallway.

Rainey turned to Janet and Ben with an expression of sheer delight.

Preston has been trying to figure out how to get Flegg into Kid Court ever since we started, and I actually did it. I mean . . . *we* actually did it.

You're a genius, Ben!

Ben tried to smile, but all he could think about was what Flegg had said. If things weren't going to change, what was the point?

"Come on," said Rainey. "We have so much work to do."

"What do you mean?" asked Ben.

"Tell your witnesses to meet us at Buckets and Barlow at four p.m. sharp. Don't be late. We have a trial to prepare for."

CHAPTER 23

After school, Ben and Janet climbed onto Jalopy and clanked their way downtown. They lost the front fender to a pothole on St. James. Then one of Ben's pedals snapped off as they made the turn onto High Street.

Ben had scooted past the law offices of Buckets and Barlow a thousand times or more, but he'd never stopped to look until today.

He was enchanted by the dark wooden door, its gleaming brass knob, and the sparkling window etched with an old-fashioned scale, the kind with two shallow bowls hanging side by side.

A few minutes later, Walter and Darby showed up on their bikes. Then the grand door swung open, and there was Rainey, waiting for them in the lobby with a huge smile on her face.

"Come in," she said. "And welcome. Who's ready for some justice?"

As they followed her down a long hallway, they ran into a woman who was just coming out of an office. Her haircut, briefcase, and blazer looked an awful lot like Rainey's.

Good afternoon, Counselor,

said Rainey with a courteous nod.

That's a fancy way of addressing a lawyer,

she explained to Ben and the others.

"Good afternoon, *Counselor*," the woman replied, trying to look serious while smiling a little. "Might you introduce me to your clients?"

"This is my plaintiff, Ben, and our star witnesses, Janet, Darby, and Walter."

Walter grinned, Darby nodded, and Janet beamed, clearly pleased to be considered a star of any kind.

"And this is my *colleague* Trudy Barlow," Rainey continued. "She's in the business of providing justice for all."

No matter how small,

said Mrs. Barlow with a grin.

That's my motto, and I'm sticking to it.

Ben liked that. Maybe he wasn't the smallest, but next to Flegg, he was a speck. "Nice to meet you," he said.

"And you," said Mrs. Barlow. "What are you all up to?"

"We have a court date tomorrow," Rainey replied. "I have to prepare the witnesses. How about you?"

"I have to write a brief and file a motion and then, to celebrate, write another brief."

YAY

YAY!

YAY!

Keep up the good fight, said Rainey.

For now, we must run. Good afternoon, Counselor.

Carry on, Counselor.

Mrs. Barlow gave Rainey a respectful nod before continuing her purposeful march down the hallway.

"Was that . . . your mom?" Janet asked. Ben could tell she was impressed.

"*Technically* speaking, yes," Rainey replied. "But within these walls, I prefer to think of her as my associate."

"She seems nice," said Ben. He wanted to say she seemed nice and smart and strong and fierce and inspiring, but he thought it might be weird to use so many adjectives.

"It depends who you ask," Rainey replied. "In court, she's known for being a tough cookie. There's plenty of people around town who don't think she's nice at all."

"Oh yeah?" Janet was interested.

"She's not afraid to pick fights in the name of justice. Some lawyers won't take cases unless there's big money involved. Mom will represent anyone she believes in."

Ben liked that.

Rainey led them down the hallway and into a room with an extremely long table lined with luxurious leather chairs.

They sat down, and Rainey explained how the trial would work.

She would begin by telling the jury what Flegg had done.

Then Janet, Walter, and Darby would say what they'd seen.

And then Fizz would have the chance to ask them questions.

"In most trials, the defendant's lawyer will do their best to rattle the witnesses and make them look unreliable. But we don't have to worry about that with Fizz. He'll be on our side."

"Wait." Ben was confused. "Isn't he supposed to be on *Flegg's* side?"

Ben remembered Mr. P. saying that even when someone had done something wrong, their lawyer would still try as hard as possible to explain their side of the situation.

"Right," said Rainey, realizing Ben had caught her saying the wrong thing. "Of *course* Fizz is on Flegg's side. All I meant was, since everyone in the jury already knows Flegg is guilty, whatever Fizz asks won't make any difference. You guys don't have anything to worry about."

"Okay," said Ben. Rainey seemed sure.

"For now, I'm going to ask you witnesses some practice questions to give you a sense of how it's going to work."

Got it, said Janet.

Great, said Walter.

Fire away, said Darby.

What should I do? Ben asked.

Sit tight for now, Rainey replied.

"I have to go to the bathroom," said Ben. It wasn't true, and he didn't feel like sitting tight. He felt pinched and restless. "Down the hall to your right," said Rainey. On his way to the bathroom, Ben passed Mrs. Barlow's office. Her door was open, and her desk was a mess, piled high with folders and coffee mugs and empty takeout containers. He paused for a second and marveled. It was like a hurricane frozen in time. He didn't think Mrs. Barlow even noticed he was there. But he was wrong.

Come in, she said without looking up.

Have a seat.

"I was just . . . I mean . . ." Ben didn't want to interrupt.

Mrs. Barlow clicked her pen twice and looked up at Ben. "You're full of questions. Maybe I have answers. *Sit.*"

Ben sat. He hadn't realized he was full of questions, but Mrs. Barlow was right.

"You're nervous about tomorrow."

"Yeah."

"*Why?* Rainey tells me your case is a no-brainer."

Ben wasn't sure why.

"You're worried about this bully and what he might do?"

Ben nodded. "Rainey told you about the case?"

"We lawyers sometimes talk amongst ourselves."

There in the clutter on the desk, Ben noticed a little scale that looked like the one etched into the front window. "What *is* that?"

"The scales of justice. Do you know what justice is?"

"*Sort* of."

"Think of it this way: When things are good between two people, the two sides of the scale are evenly balanced, like they are right now. But when someone puts their needs above someone else's, things get out of whack." Mrs. Barlow pressed down on one side of the scale, which caused the other side to rise.

"Right now, my finger is Flegg. By stealing your cookies, he's messing with the balance of justice."

That made sense to Ben. He'd been feeling a little crooked lately.

"Rainey is trying to help you get things *back* in balance." Mrs. Barlow lifted her finger, and the Flegg side and the Ben side were even again.

"That sounds good," said Ben. "But I'm not sure it's possible."

You want to know a secret about bullies?

Yes!

Ben leaned forward. It was like she was reading his mind.

"People pick on other people for all sorts of reasons. But usually they're trying to make themselves feel better."

"Better about what?"

"It's different for everyone. Being a person is hard. Most bullies I've met don't even want to be bullies. It's just that they don't know any other way to get what they want."

Ben thought about that. He usually got what he wanted by being nice. Was it possible Flegg didn't know how?

"Does it work?" he asked.

"Does *what* work?"

"Does taking my cookies make Flegg feel better?"

"Maybe for a while. That's why he keeps doing it. But it probably doesn't fix his actual problem."

"How do you fix his actual problem?"

"I have no idea what his actual problem is," she replied, glancing at Ben over the top of her glasses. "I'm trying to fix *yours*."

"Oh!" said Ben. "Yes, please."

"Bullies try to make you think they're in charge by using whatever kind of strength they have. To fight back, you have to use the kind of strength *you* have."

What kind of strength do I have?

"I don't know," said Mrs. Barlow with a sideways smile. "I just met you."

"Right." Ben was disappointed. For some reason, he'd expected her to have the answer. "How do you know so much about bullies, anyway?"

"Because I spend most of my time taking them to court, and . . ." Mrs. Barlow looked Ben right in the eye.

Because I used to be one.

She said it so matter-of-factly that it caught Ben off guard. "What?" He wasn't sure he'd heard correctly.

"It's true! I was really good at cutting people down. That was my strength. I scared people into doing exactly what I wanted."

"What made you change?"

I had a kid. And it made me realize something that turned my world upside down.

What?

I was even *better* at building people up. Using my strength to help people was a lot more fun. So I got a new motto.

"What was your old motto?"

"I didn't really have one, to be honest, but it would have been something like

JUSTICE for SOME."

"I prefer your new one."

"Me too. I'm a better lawyer now. And a better mom. But I still don't always get it right. You want to know what's hardest for me now?"

"Sure."

"Not going too far in the opposite direction." Mrs. Barlow pressed her finger on the other side of the scale.

Now the Ben side went down and the Flegg side rose up.

"This might *feel* good. But that doesn't make it *fair*. Do you know what I mean?"

"Yeah," said Ben, nodding, though he wasn't entirely sure.

"Good," she said with a nod that suggested she was done saying wise things and ready to get back to work.

"I should go," said Ben. Rainey was probably wondering where he was.

Mrs. Barlow nodded again and picked up her pen. Ben headed off, still searching for answers. He didn't find them in the bathroom.

By the time he got back to the conference room, Rainey was finishing up.

That's it, she said.

Eat a good dinner. Get some sleep. And be sure to dress snappy tomorrow. This is the moment to pull out your finest.

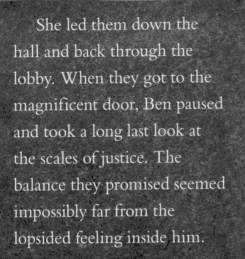

She led them down the
hall and back through the
lobby. When they got to the
magnificent door, Ben paused
and took a long last look at
the scales of justice. The
balance they promised seemed
impossibly far from the
lopsided feeling inside him.

CHAPTER 24

The next morning, Ben put on his best tie. It was his only tie. Which also made it his worst tie. And his itchiest tie. But also his least itchy tie.

While Ben stared in the mirror doing a terrible job of tying the knot, he thought about the trial and wondered whether it would turn out to be the best day of his life or the worst.

When he got to the corner with the yellow
bush, Janet was already there wearing what
seemed to be a wedding dress
that had just lost a
fight with a panther.

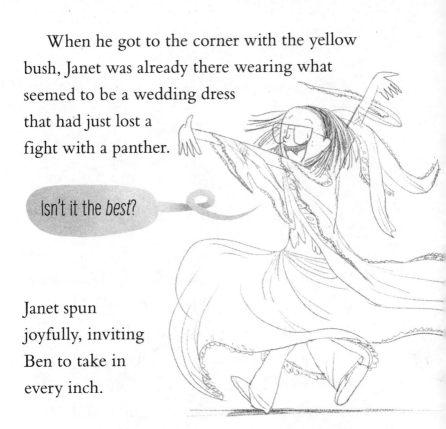

Isn't it the *best?*

Janet spun
joyfully, inviting
Ben to take in
every inch.

The lace was torn and the satin was frayed.
Janet's purple pajamas peeked out through several
gaping holes. Ben didn't know much about
fashion, but he was pretty sure this wasn't it.

"In case you were wondering, it was *free,*"
Janet continued. "I found it by the curb last week
and hoped I'd have a good enough reason to
wear it someday. Who knew someday would
come so soon?"

Ben didn't answer. Instead, he just marveled.

Now Janet was doing leprechaun kicks.

I like how the purple shows through.

Ben tilted his head and squinted. He did kind of like how the purple showed through.

"You look nice, too," Janet gushed. "That's interesting what you did with your tie."

Ben touched his tie without meaning to. "I'm not sure I got it right," he admitted. He'd watched a how-to video on the internet. But the video had made assumptions Ben's fingers couldn't live up to.

"Whatever." Janet was radiant. "I like it. Where did you get it?"

"It was a hand-me-down."

"So it was . . . *free*?"

"I mean . . ." Ben saw he was stuck. "I *guess*."

But Janet had on a friendly smile and not a *Gotcha* one. "No *wonder* I like it so much."

As she steered Jalopy down the sidewalk, Janet beamed like the sun on a day with no clouds. Ben had never seen her this delighted. She was so convinced her dress was beautiful that, after a few blocks, he believed it, too.

CHAPTER 25

When Ben and Janet got to the four square court,
Rainey was already there, wearing a crisp blue
blazer and her hair in a bun. She looked exactly
like a smaller version of her mom. Which gave
Ben an unexpected jolt of hope.

He looked around. There were PJ and Fizz.
There were the members of the jury.

All they needed was Flegg.

He'll show up,

Rainey insisted.

He'd better,

said PJ, sucking on a
lollipop, which
seemed strangely at
odds with his shirt
and tie.

They all scanned the schoolyard. Flegg should have been easy to see. There was no crowd in which he wouldn't be the tallest.

Ben spotted him first, over by the kickball field, rolling steadily toward them like a tidal wave rising from an otherwise tranquil sea.

When Flegg finally got to the four square court, he walked over to Rainey and threw the red card at her feet. As he took his place in the circle, everyone inched anxiously away until there were person-size gaps on either side of him. Even PJ, standing in the first square, stepped back a little.

Ben wondered how it felt, always being avoided like that. Of course, it was all Flegg's fault—he drove people away with the things he did and said—but Ben guessed it felt bad all the same.

PJ crunched his lollipop and shoved the stick in his pocket. Then he picked up the ball and bounced it twice. "I hereby call to order the trial of *Ben Yokoyama v. Flegg McEggers*. We'll start by hearing from Rainey."

PJ bounced the ball to Rainey, who bounced it to Fizz, who bounced it to Ben, who was standing in the fourth square waiting to see what would happen. The ball moved back and forth like that as Rainey began.

"I'll keep it short and sweet, folks. Flegg stole Ben's cookie and fortune three days in a row. Ben wants his first fortune back."

PJ nodded and bounced the ball to Fizz. "Opening statement for the defense."

"Okay, Flegg," said Fizz. "Come take Ben's place."

Flegg stepped into the fourth square and somehow managed to glare in every direction at once.

Fizz bounced him the ball, but instead of bouncing it back, Flegg held it in his hands. "Are we having a trial or playing a game?"

"Both," said PJ.

"That's funny," said Flegg.

"What is?" PJ was impatient and uncertain. "What's funny?"

The first time I get invited to play four square, I'm not actually getting to play four square.

Instead of bouncing the ball gently to Rainey, Flegg spiked it as hard as he could, sending it high above her head.

There was a collective gasp. What Flegg had done was not just against the *rules*. It was also *rude*. It would have been hard for anyone to reach the ball, but for Rainey, it was impossible.

One of the jurors ran to get the ball and handed it back to PJ.

"I guess we'll play *three* square for now," he said, bouncing the ball to Fizz, who bounced it to Rainey, who bounced it back to PJ while Flegg just stood there, inside his square but outside the game.

"Opening statements for the defense," PJ repeated.

Fizz held the ball and cleared his throat.

Look,

I'm not going to tell you Flegg doesn't sometimes eat cookies and candy that started the day in someone else's lunch box. Sometimes he does. But most of the time he's just *suggesting* that people give them their cookies. He's not *taking* them, exactly.

Thank you,

said PJ.

Rainey, call your first witness.

"I call Janet Everly," said Rainey.

Janet jumped eagerly into the fourth square, and Flegg shuffled out. There was a gasp when the jury got its first good look at her dress.

"Janet, please tell us—" Rainey began.

But Janet didn't need any prompting. "I have witnessed Flegg take Ben's cookies *three days in a row.*"

Janet's gaze was as sharp and fierce as a pirate's dagger.

"Thank you, Janet," said Rainey, bouncing the ball to Janet. "Did Ben *willingly* give his cookies to Flegg, as Fizz has suggested?"

"Heck no! Ben *begged* Flegg not to take them!"

"No further questions, Your Honor," said Rainey.

Which meant it was Fizz's turn.

"You say you *saw* Flegg take Ben's cookies?" he asked Janet.

"I sure did."

"Very interesting," said Fizz. "Is it possible you *mistook* my client for someone else? How can the jury be sure your eyesight is good enough to correctly identify him?"

Janet removed her headband and threw it at Fizz, bonking him lightly in the middle of his forehead.

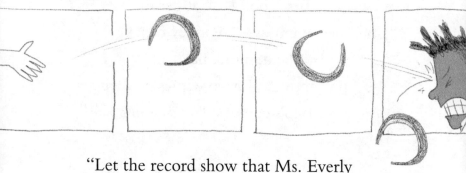

"Let the record show that Ms. Everly sees quite well," said Rainey.

"Noted," said PJ. "Janet has excellent aim."

"No further questions," said Fizz, bouncing the ball back to Rainey.

"Next I call Walter Stillman, Your Honor," said Rainey.

PJ bounced the ball to Walter, and Walter bounced it back. "This is fun," he said, laughing.

"No laughing in Kid Court," said PJ. "This is serious business."

Sorry, said Walter. I'll be extremely serious.

But Walter kept smiling anyway.

"Did you see Flegg take Ben's cookies?" asked Rainey.

"Yes. Two days ago before school and also the morning before that. Do I have to throw something at Fizz?"

"That won't be necessary," said Fizz. "But I have a question. Has Flegg ever taken your cookies?"

"Every day."

"*Including* today?"

"Yes. This morning before school."

"Did he take them, or . . . did you *give* them to him?"

"I mean . . . well . . . I *did* give them to him today."

"Could you say that again . . . to the *jury*?"

"I gave them to him today, but before that, he definitely *took* them."

"Let the record show that Walter just admitted to *giving* his cookies to Flegg."

"It is noted that Walter's snickerdoodles were freely given," PJ replied.

"Wait! That's not what I'm saying." Walter was crestfallen.

"No further questions, Your Honor," said Fizz.

"I call Darby Washington," said Rainey, who seemed rattled and flustered.

Walter shuffled back to the circle as Darby took his spot in the fourth square.

"Am I correct that you are a certified math genius?" asked Rainey.

Darby blushed. "I've studied with Professor Charles Washington, head of the Department of Mathematics at Honeycutt University."

"And you have some findings to share?"

Yes, Darby replied.

I talked to twenty kids at Honeycutt and used their responses to determine that sixty-five percent of our fellow students have had their desserts stolen by Flegg at some point this year. That's one hundred and sixty-five students.

Rainey gave a dramatic gasp and glanced at the jury. "So, in addition to taking my client's cookies, Flegg has committed similar crimes against *more than half* of the school?"

"That's what the numbers suggest."

"Shocking," said Rainey, looking over at the jury and shaking her head disapprovingly. "Utterly *shocking*."

She bounced the ball to Fizz, who bounced it to Darby.

"Did you actually *talk* to one hundred and sixty-five students?" Fizz asked.

No. I derived that number from a random sample. It's a widely accepted process that stands up to every standard of statistical analysis.

Speak English!

Fizz insisted.

Darby cleared his throat. "If you talk to a few people, you can use their answers to figure out how a larger group would probably answer the same questions."

"This is a court of law," said Fizz, glancing over at the jury with exaggerated outrage. "We deal in *facts*. Not probabilities!"

The numbers don't lie, Darby insisted.

But maybe *you* do?

Excuse me? Darby was offended.

OBJECTION! Rainey shouted.

No further questions, Your Honor, said Fizz.

Rainey rolled over to where Ben was standing. She must have realized how uneasy he was feeling. "It's going to be okay. Fizz is just doing his job. A little too well, if you ask me, but our case is ironclad, and the jury knows it."

Ben tried his hardest to smile.

"Does the defense have any witnesses?" asked PJ.

"Nope," said Fizz. "My client's innocence is obvious."

"Closing arguments, then."

Rainey cleared her throat and straightened her blazer. Ben could tell she was worried but trying not to show it.

"Eyewitnesses have confirmed what you all know. Flegg took Ben's cookies and stole his fortune. What's more, as our expert witness testified, nearly two-thirds of your fellow students have also been hassled by Flegg. In the name of justice, I ask you to find Flegg McEggers guilty and end his reign of terror."

Janet burst into applause.

PJ scowled. "Please restrain your witness. We do not clap in Kid Court."

"Sorry!" said Janet, who immediately stopped clapping but definitely wasn't sorry.

"Closing arguments for the defense," said PJ.

"This is pretty simple," said Fizz. "Ben's entire case rests on the word of his strangely dressed friend, a kid who admitted to *giving* his cookies to Flegg, and someone who's trying to fool you with fake numbers."

RUDE!

WAIT...

HEY!

"Objection!" said Rainey.

"I'm just quoting your witnesses," Fizz insisted.

"Overruled," said PJ. "Actually, I think your arguments are pretty persuasive, Fizz."

"You do?" Fizz seemed surprised.

"I do," said PJ. "In my opinion, Rainey failed to present a shred of actual evidence. Which is why I've decided to bypass the jury and rule on this case myself."

Ben didn't understand what was happening, but he could tell from the look on Rainey's face that it wasn't good.

Wait,

said Rainey, who seemed more stunned than mad.

That's not how it works.

It works how I *say* it works,

PJ fired back.

I'm chief justice. And I find Flegg not guilty.

Rainey gasped.

Fizz just stood there with his mouth open.

The various members of the jury exchanged glances of confusion and surprise. Flegg laughed and kept laughing like the alarm that blares when something on the stove is burning and the kitchen fills up with smoke.

211

CHAPTER 26

The next thing Ben heard was Rainey shouting.
"What in the world's gotten into you, Preston?
You can't *do* this!"

"I *can,*" said PJ in a cold, commanding voice.
"I just did."

Rainey rolled herself over to the jury.

I don't know what's going on, but this isn't
how it works. You, the jury, have a right to
rule on Ben's case. You have a *duty.*

But the members
of the jury wouldn't
meet her eyes.

squealed Janet
with glee.

All eyes turned to look at Janet, who was holding a lollipop in one hand and a backpack in the other.

"That's mine," snarled PJ, lurching toward her. "Give it back."

"In a minute," she said, running around the four square court while PJ raced after her. As she jogged along, Janet pulled treats out of the backpack and tossed them into the air.

Cookies, candy, granola bars, little cups of lunch box pudding.

"There are an awful lot of desserts in here, PJ."

"I like desserts," he shouted back. "I'm allowed to have as many as I want."

"That may be true," said Janet between heaving breaths. "But what I can't figure out is how you knew the kind of cookie Flegg stole from Walter, since Walter never even mentioned snickerdoodles."

"Of course he did," PJ objected.

213

"You're right. He *didn't*!" gasped Rainey, like someone who just remembered how to spell a long and tricky word.

"Then how would PJ know unless . . ." Janet reached into the backpack, grabbed a bag of snickerdoodles, and held it high above her head for all to see. "Unless . . ." And then she paused as the clues clicked into place and the shocking conclusion became clear.

He was *conspiring* with Flegg!

With a quick flick of her wrist, Janet tossed the bag to Rainey, who caught it with one hand.

"I submit this evidence to the court," Rainey declared.

"Hold on, Peej," Fizz demanded. "What's going on?"

"Those are mine," said PJ. "I swear."

"Look inside the bag," said Walter. "My mom always puts a note in with my cookies. Sometimes she even makes puns."

Rainey pulled out a folded piece of paper. She read the note out loud.

Walter—
Here's a treat as sweet as you are.
Love,
Mom

"That note is from *my* mom," PJ declared triumphantly.

Dear Walter
Here's a treat as sweet as you are.
Love,
mom

Then why does it say "Dear Walter" at the top?

Rainey fired back.

PJ stopped dead in his tracks.

"Look!" said Rainey, wheeling over to Fizz and showing him the note. "Did you know about this?"

Fizz read the note and then glared at PJ. "Explain yourself."

But PJ didn't.

"What did you *do*, Preston?" Rainey was furious and heartbroken. Ben could tell she was close to tears.

"Look at me!" she insisted.

But PJ wouldn't look.

"I submit this evidence," said Rainey, rolling over to the jury and holding up the note. "For whatever reason, Preston has betrayed us. This case was rigged. But you can still fix it!"

Ben looked at the jury and saw a sea of faces knotted with confusion and fear. They all knew Flegg was guilty. They all knew PJ had done something unthinkable.

Ben had a sense
that if they just
talked things through,
they'd realize they were
actually on the same page.
That there were enough of
them to do the right thing.
But no one was willing to speak first.

Because PJ was standing right there.
Because he was in charge.
Because no one wanted to make him mad.
PJ's expression was cruel and defiant. In that
moment, he looked like someone else Ben knew.
In that moment, he looked a lot like Flegg.

That's what I thought, said PJ.

The jury agrees. My ruling
stands. Flegg is innocent.

Rainey spun around to face PJ, her indignation
rising into rage.

Why did you do this?

She could hardly find the words, she was so mad.

Because you wanted . . .
cookies? *Answer* me, Preston!

Why do you call me Preston?

PJ was flustered.

Stop calling me that.

Don't change the subject,

Rainey snapped back.

Answer the question.

Everyone was staring at PJ now. Fizz,
the witnesses, the jury, Flegg. Everyone
wanted to hear what he had to say.

"Okay, fine," said PJ like he was the one
who'd been wronged. "Flegg gave me those
cookies. But I don't even *like* cookies."

"Then why did you do it?" Rainey was
practically spitting the words.

PJ ignored her. He turned to the jury as if he
were the person on trial. "Listen, folks. Flegg
promised that if I found him not guilty, he'd leave
everyone in Four Square Club alone for the rest of
the year. No more stolen stuff. No more hassles."

"I sure hope you mean everyone in the school," said Rainey pointedly.

"No," PJ admitted. "But everyone in Four Square Club. Even *you*."

Rainey swallowed back tears and took a deep breath. She sat high in her seat and looked at PJ with eyes that were angry but still clinging to the thinnest thread of hope.

"I understand wanting to get Flegg off your back. I *get* it. *Sort* of. But . . . you care about *justice,* Preston." Rainey spoke gently, as if trying to help him remember. "*That's* why I call you Preston, because PJ seems like too small a name to hold all the *good* things inside you. *That's* why you helped me start Kid Court, right? Because you care so much about the Code of the Schoolyard?"

PJ's face got mean and sharp, like a hatchet looking for a branch to lop off.

There *is* no Code of the Schoolyard,

he sneered.

That's made-up kid stuff, Rainey. And I only did Kid Court to get some practice so I can try out for the academy debate team.

Rainey looked like someone who's been stabbed in the back but refuses to admit it hurts.

"But . . . what you're doing isn't *justice*, Preston." Her guard was down. Her heart was out in the open for anyone to look at or step on. "It's just plain . . . *wrong*."

PJ scoffed. "Justice isn't a matter of right and wrong, Rainey. It's about who's standing in the first square."

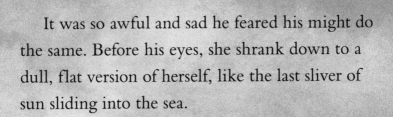

Ben saw it, the moment Rainey's heart broke.

It was so awful and sad he feared his might do the same. Before his eyes, she shrank down to a dull, flat version of herself, like the last sliver of sun sliding into the sea.

Her dream had turned into a nightmare. Her hero was actually the worst kind of villain.

Ben still wasn't sure what justice *was* exactly, but what PJ had done was the opposite.

"You're wrong," said Rainey in a voice clear and true. And then she stopped shrinking and started getting bigger again. "Clearly, this is just a game to you all." She pointed at PJ and then at the jury. "You go ahead and play four square. I'm leaving and taking Kid Court with me."

You can't do that.

PJ was indignant.

It's *mine*.

It was only ever half yours . . . *PJ,*

replied Rainey coolly.

I'm taking your half back. If you have a problem with that, I'd be happy to tell the people at Honeycutt Academy that their new star debater is a lying, cheating, selfish jerkball who's just as small as his nickname.

You . . . wouldn't,

said PJ like he'd just been kicked where it hurts the most.

— HIYAAA!

I really should. But I probably won't. As long as you never come near me again.

It seemed PJ had run out of things to say.

"Come with me," said Rainey, wheeling herself away from the four square court.

"Who?" asked Ben, who wasn't sure of anything at the moment.

"You, Janet, Walter, Darby. Anyone with a shred of self-respect."

"What about me?" Fizz asked like he wasn't sure.

Rainey shot him a look like a sideways icicle. "Were you in on this?"

I wasn't. I *swear*. PJ told me to go hard on your witnesses, that's all.

"If you were actually defending your client, I respect that. But if you're okay with what PJ did, then you're no better than he is."

Fizz was clearly torn. He looked over at PJ, trying to decide what to do.

Rainey didn't wait to find out.

"You too, Flegg," she barked with impatience. "Follow me. We're not done."

I'm not coming with you,

said Flegg, like the only tree standing after a forest fire.

Didn't you hear what PJ said? I *won*.

"Sorry, Flegg," said Rainey. "But you bribed the wrong judge. Either you're coming with me or I'm going to Principal Hogan. Your choice."

Flegg scowled in defeat and followed along behind Ben and the others, who were trying to keep up with Rainey as she raced across the schoolyard.

225

Where are we going?

asked Ben, jogging
along beside her.

I'm not sure yet. But we have a
trial to finish, and I need a jury.

Ben saw a spark in her eye as she suddenly
changed direction and headed toward the
far back corner of the
schoolyard.

Good news, she announced.

I've figured out *exactly* where we're headed.

Where?
asked Ben, who felt hopelessly lost and badly in need of a new destination.

To the future.

Follow me.

 At that moment, Ben would have followed her anywhere.

CHAPTER 27

Rainey rolled over to a patch of grass where a group of kindergartners were kicking a ball back and forth.

It was the Junior Kickball Club, Ben realized. Little kids who wanted to play but weren't quite ready to join the main game.

Excuse me for a moment, said Rainey in a voice that was commanding and certain.

Gather around, everyone.

The kindergartners were surprised at first, and then they were curious. When one of them pointed out that Rainey was a fourth grader, they rushed over as if a movie star had suddenly appeared.

"Do you guys know about the Code of the Schoolyard?" Rainey asked.

The response was a sea of shaking heads.

"Well, you *should*," said Rainey. "The code tells us to all treat each other kindly and fairly. To admit it when we make mistakes. And to do our best to fix things when we mess them up."

"That makes sense," said a kindergartner named Martha. "Is that it?"

Ben knew her name was Martha because it was knitted into her sweater.

"Pretty much," said Rainey.

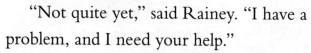

Can we go now?

asked Martha.

It's my turn to kick.

"Not quite yet," said Rainey. "I have a problem, and I need your help."

"Did you pee in your pants?" asked Martha.

"Nope," said Rainey, trying to hide her smile. "The *problem* is that someone might have broken the code, and we need to find out for sure."

"Noah peed in his pants earlier," Martha said, pointing at a boy with a red sweater and a buzz cut.

It was an accident,

said Noah, nodding.

"I'll help you," said Martha, looking at Rainey.

"Me too," said Noah.

"Thanks, guys," said Rainey. "How about the rest of you?"

The various kindergartners responded with a jumbled assortment of words that meant yes. They were eager and excited. This was even better than kickball.

Rainey turned to Ben and Janet and Walter and Darby with a look of determination. "All right, folks. We have a jury. I'm the new judge. Janet, you'll be Ben's lawyer."

"What? *Me?*" Janet was pleased. "But I have no idea—"

"Here," said Rainey, handing Janet her briefcase. "This is all you really need."

Janet took the briefcase and immediately started practicing her lawyer poses.

"And now we need someone to represent Flegg," said Rainey, surveying her options.

I'll do it.

Fizz had just arrived, breathless from his sprint across the schoolyard.

"You're late," said Rainey, attempting a stern expression but obviously happy to see him.

"It looks like I'm right on time," said Fizz with a cautious grin.

"Listen up," said Rainey, speaking louder than Ben had ever heard her speak before. "We're not going to play four square. We're not going to play kickball. We're just going to have a trial. We're going to state the facts and let the people decide."

Rainey spoke like she was right where she belonged. Like she'd waited forever to fill these shoes and found they fit her perfectly.

Rainey straightened her blazer and began. "The Honorable Rainey Barlow calls this session of Kid Court to order. In the interest of time, let's skip the formalities. Opening statements, go!"

Janet took out her awful sunglasses and slid them on dramatically.

And then she paced back and forth in front of the jury, trying, Ben assumed, to look like the lawyers she'd seen on TV.

"Recess ends in five minutes!" said Rainey, tapping her watch.

"Right," said Janet, snapping to attention. She looked over at the kindergartners. "This is Ben. He's pretty great. But he's mad because that guy took his cookies." Janet pointed to Flegg.

Not cool,

said Martha.

"No chitchat from the jury please, thank you," said Rainey, shooting Martha some side-eye. Martha shot some right back. "That's all," said Janet. "Go ahead, Fizz."

"Okay, you guys," said Fizz. "This is Flegg. He loves cookies. Sometimes he takes cookies that aren't his. But I don't think he can help it, because cookies are so delicious."

Noah stood up and flung his arms wide, like he was hugging the world.

I love cookies!

Sit down, Noah, said Martha.

The judge said no chitchat.

Noah sat down fast. Martha was not to be trifled with.

"But you have to ask before you take someone's cookies," said a girl with bright green glasses and an orange jumper.

"It's not nice to just *take* them," said a boy with black hair and no front teeth.

"Let the record show that these jurors seem to understand the Code of the Schoolyard *perfectly*," said Janet.

"Noted," said Rainey. "Three minutes!
Present your witnesses. *Quickly.*"

"This is Walter," said Janet. "Walter, did you
see Flegg take Ben's cookies?"

Yeah. I did,

said Walter.

I definitely did.

"How about you, Darby?"

Yep.

"That's all I've got," said Janet.

"Are there any witnesses for the defense?"
asked Rainey.

"Nope," said Fizz.

"Wait," said Noah. "Yesterday that big guy helped me get my ball out of a tree." He was pointing at Flegg.

"He did?" Rainey was surprised.

"Yeah. He was nice."

Rainey looked over at Flegg. "Is this true?"

Flegg nodded, almost like he didn't want to admit it.

"Let the record show that Flegg did something nice," said Fizz.

"Noted," said Rainey, who seemed slightly conflicted. "Closing statements."

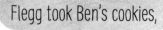

Flegg took Ben's cookies,

said Janet.

But at least once, he did something nice,

said Fizz.

"What makes you so sure?" asked Rainey.

"I saw him do it," said Martha.

"We were standing right there," said Noah, nodding.

"Thanks, guys," said Rainey. "You can go back to your game. Let the record show that the jury has found Flegg guilty of taking Ben's cookies."

"Big deal," said Flegg. "So what?"

"A jury of your peers has spoken, Flegg. Before I deliver your sentence, I'm giving you one last chance to give Ben back his fortune. That's all he's asking."

Ben couldn't believe that after everything Flegg had done, Rainey was still trying so hard to be fair.

But Flegg crossed his arms and shook his head. In a way, Ben admired him for sticking to his guns.

"All right, then," said Rainey with a look of fierce determination. "You've left me no choice. You took Ben's fortune, which he was going to use to get a new scooter. I hereby sentence you, Flegg McEggers, to surrender your Astrostar to Ben."

"What?" Ben was shocked. It wasn't what he'd expected to hear.

No way,

said Flegg.

He'd been mostly silent and still throughout the trial, but Rainey's verdict woke something inside him.

I shoveled sidewalks all winter to make enough to buy that scooter. I worked real hard. This isn't fair.

Rainey gave Flegg a look that might have knocked Ben over if it had been pointed at him.

"Don't talk to me about *fairness,* Flegg," she thundered. "Was it *fair* when you took Ben's cookies? Is it *fair* that you've stolen things from so many of us? Is it *fair* that we have to worry where you are at any given time? Look at me, Flegg!"

But Flegg wouldn't look. He stared at the ground.

Rainey rolled over and glared straight up into Flegg's downcast eyes. He towered above her, but she was the one who seemed taller.

Is it *fair* when you call me "Wheelchair"? I have a name, Flegg, and it's *Lorraine*!

Flegg looked to the side.

Maybe your life isn't fair, but neither is mine! I'm trying my hardest to make things as fair as possible, and you are definitely not helping!

Look at me, Flegg!

Flegg looked at Rainey, but only for a second.
Ben guessed it felt like looking at the sun.

241

Rainey wheeled herself away and gave Flegg some room. She took a deep breath, and when she continued talking, she sounded like a judge again. "You can accept your sentence, or we can talk to Principal Hogan. Your choice."

Flegg slumped. He had no good options, and he knew it.

Fine, he said in a quiet rage.

Whatever.

He turned and started walking straight toward Ben, his fists clenched and his face full of fury.

Ben closed his eyes.
Whatever was about to happen,
he didn't want to see it.

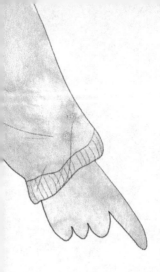

CHAPTER 28

Ben waited for the world to end, but it didn't.

"Everything's okay, Ben." It was Janet. Her
voice was calm.

Ben opened his eyes. Flegg was halfway
across the schoolyard.

"Look," said Martha, pointing at
the ground in front of Ben. "The
big boy dropped it."

Ben looked down.
At his feet was a key. The
kind that fits into a bike lock.

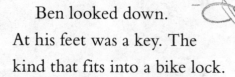

Before Ben's brain could make sense
of everything that had just happened,
a whole new something began.

There was Ms. Mung, with a curious look on
her face. "What's going on over here? I thought
you were going to play four square with Flegg."

 Ben's brain was an
empty slate, but he picked
up some chalk and started
to scribble.

"We played four square *first*. And then Flegg
gave me back my fortune." It was sort of a lie,
but it also sort of wasn't.

"Well, that's wonderful," said Ms. Mung,
smiling. "And now . . . ?" She looked down at
Martha, who was hugging Janet's leg. "You're
playing with the *first graders*?"

"Kindergartners!" said Martha, who was
clearly offended.

"We sure are," said Ben. There was no point
denying it.

They're so much fun,

said Janet, trying to sound
like someone who's having
so much fun.

We were playing Kid Corks, said Martha proudly.

It's the Coat of the Schoolyard.

That's wonderful, sweetheart. Good for *you*,

said Ms. Mung in the voice adults use to talk to kindergartners who aren't making any sense.

So everything's okay between you and Flegg?

she asked, looking at Ben.

"Definitely," he answered. But this part was less clear.

"Well, I'm glad you thought of that solution," said Ms. Mung. "I have to admit, I wasn't sure it was going to work."

"Me neither," said Ben, who'd been skeptical himself.

But . . . it *had* worked. *Hadn't* it?

Ben had gotten what he wanted, and technically, he hadn't had to pay for it. But for whatever reason, the key in his hand felt incredibly heavy.

Ms. Mung headed off to some other part of the schoolyard, leaving Ben standing there wondering.

"We did it," said Rainey, beaming and proud. "One injustice down. A million more to go."

"Are you going to keep doing Kid Court?" Ben asked.

"Of course."

"But what about the rest of the club? Don't you need a jury?"

"Yes, but I realized something. The jury should never be part of the club. It should always just be regular kids."

"Don't you need lawyers?" asked Janet.

"Count me in," said Fizz.

"Great, and I was hoping *you* might be interested," said Rainey, shooting Janet a cheerful smile. "You're a *natural*."

"Of course I am," Janet agreed. "But . . . I'm only in third grade."

"That's okay!" said Rainey. "The Code of the Schoolyard only works if *everyone* knows about it."

"But if everyone knows, won't Principal Hogan find out?" Ben wondered.

Rainey gave him a playful grin. "*PJ* is the one who tried to talk Principal Hogan into letting us do Kid Court. I like my chances of persuading him."

Ben liked her chances, too. He wouldn't want to get into an argument with Rainey.

"Well then, I'm in," said Janet. "I'm not sure if you heard, Ben, but I'm a *natural*."

"She really is," Fizz agreed.

Recess was over. Kids started lining up to go back inside. Walter and Darby headed off together, and Janet walked over to talk to Kamari.

"Thanks, Rainey," said Ben. Of all the emotions swirling inside him, gratitude was loudest.

"Thank *you,* Ben. I'm glad you got your scooter, but I got my swagger back. I hadn't even realized it was missing."

Rainey picked up her briefcase and smiled.

Justice has been served!

she shouted in triumph as she rolled herself away.

But Ben wasn't sure about that.

CHAPTER 29

After school, Ben rushed outside and hid behind a bush. He didn't know how things stood with Flegg, and he wasn't ready to find out.

Ben watched as Flegg appeared and glanced miserably at the Astrostar before shuffling off glumly down the sidewalk.

Once Flegg was safely out of sight, Ben walked over to the Astrostar. There it was. Shiny and perfect and finally *his*.

He took out the key and unlocked the chain. Nothing could stop him from taking a ride.

Janet walked over with a smile of admiration.

"Well, Ben, it looks like your fortune worked after all. I'm happy for you."

CLICK!

But Janet's mood didn't match her words.

"What's wrong?" Ben asked.

"Let's just say I've had better days. While we were in school, Jalopy seems to have bit the dust."

Ben followed her brokenhearted gaze to the far end of the bike rack. There was Jalopy in various pieces. He tried to feel sad for Janet's sake. "I'll help you put her back together."

"No, Ben," said Janet. "We must face the hard truth. Jalopy's time has come. She brought us joy. She gave us her best. But now we have to let her go."

"To the dump?"

"Probably. But I prefer to think of it as the great big sidewalk in the sky."

Ben lowered his head and said nothing. It seemed like the only appropriate response.

"Now go." Janet was putting on a brave face. "I need some time to say my farewells. Plus, this is the moment you've been waiting for. Take that scooter for a spin."

Ben nodded and gave a farewell wave to Jalopy. As he hopped onto the Astrostar and sped smoothly down the sidewalk, the awfulness of his broken old scooter was a vague and distant memory.

Ben rode around the long loop in the park and then did it again.

The Astrostar was everything he'd dreamed. But as Ben sped along, finally free of the *thump thump thump*ing of his dented tire, all he could hear was the *thump thump thump*ing of his aching heart. He told his heart to be quiet, but it *thump*ed even louder in response.

Ben hoped he'd get home in time to stash the scooter somewhere before his parents saw it. He wasn't ready to explain where it had come from. But when he turned the corner onto his block, the green car was just pulling into the driveway.

Ben's dad popped out with a smile on his face.

Is this your new scooter, Ben? What a beauty! I'm so proud of you for saving your birthday money.

Me too,

said his mom, who had just walked out of the garage.

I didn't think you'd be able to do it.

Ben felt guilty.

He felt relieved.

The two mixed together about as nicely as ice cream and vinegar.

"Thanks," he said. "I'm going to get started on my homework."

"Sounds good," said his mom. "Dinner's in fifteen minutes."

Ben went upstairs and got in bed. He didn't feel well. He wasn't sure what to do.

He thought about the scales on the window of Buckets and Barlow.

Flegg had taken Ben's cookies, which had tilted things toward Flegg. So Ben had taken Flegg's scooter to get things back in balance. Had it worked? Were the two sides even now? Or had things tipped too far in the other direction?

As the questions piled up, one thing was clear: the Astrostar hadn't been free after all.

Ben knew what he needed to do. He just really didn't want to.

That's when the doorbell rang.

CHAPTER 30

Ben rushed down the stairs to answer the door, but his parents had gotten there first.

On the porch stood Flegg and a woman who couldn't possibly have been his mom, because she was just too small.

Ben, said Ben's mom.

Ben? said Ben's dad.

This is the boy who took your scooter? said the woman next to Flegg.

Flegg nodded sullenly and wouldn't look at Ben.

"*Ben!* What do you have to say for yourself?" his mom scolded.

"You owe Flegg an apology," said his dad.

Ben had a lot to figure out all at once.

"I'd *like* to apologize to Flegg," said Ben. "But I'd prefer to do it *privately,* if you don't mind. It's super embarrassing to apologize in front of parents."

"Is that all right with you, Flegg?" asked Ben's mom in a voice that was careful and kind.

"Yeah," said Flegg. "I don't want Ben to be embarrassed."

"That's really nice of you, Flegg," said Ben's dad.

The three grown-ups played a game of hot potato with their uneasy glances.

"How about a cup of tea while the boys talk?" Ben's mom suggested.

"Is it *good* tea?" asked Flegg's mom skeptically.

"Oh, it's our very *best* tea," said Ben's mom as they went inside. Ben knew they only had one kind.

Flegg sat on one wobbly plastic porch chair, and Ben sat on the other. He had absolutely no idea what was going to happen.

For a while, *nothing* did. They sat there as a black car drove past and, a few minutes later, a yellow one.

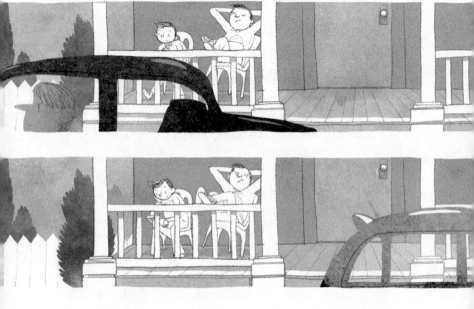

Flegg broke the silence first. "It took me so long to walk home from school that I was late. When Mom asked where my scooter was, I told her you stole it. I didn't know what else to say."

Ben wanted to be mad, but he understood. He didn't want to tell his parents the entire truth, either.

He thought he knew a way to get them both out of the pickle they were in. "I'll give your Astrostar back," he said. "I was going to anyway."

"Why?" Flegg seemed confused. And suspicious.

"Because . . . it's *yours*."

"Then why did you take it in the first place?"

Ben had been wondering the same thing. There wasn't just one answer.

"Because Rainey went to all that trouble. And because I was mad. And because I wanted you to see what it felt like to lose something."

They sat there for a minute as a kid just learning how to ride a skateboard lurched awkwardly down the sidewalk in front of Ben's house.

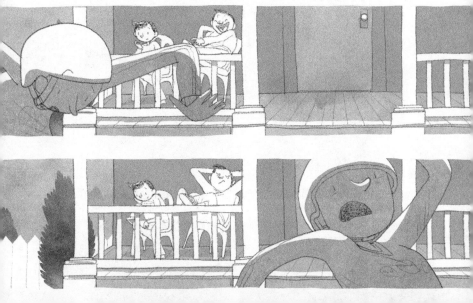

"I've lost lots of things," said Flegg. "I didn't have to learn what it feels like from you."

"Oh," said Ben, feeling bad again. "Like what?"

"I don't want to talk about it," Flegg snapped.

"Okay."

They sat there a while longer while Ben scraped together all the courage he could find.

"If I give your scooter back, will you give me back my fortune?"

"You already said you'd give it back," Flegg argued.

"I *will* give it back," said Ben. "Whether you give me my fortune or not. And whether you stop taking my cookies or not. But I'd really *like* my fortune back. And I'd really *like* you to stop taking my cookies."

"I don't have your fortune," said Flegg, sounding embarrassed.

You actually lost it?

Sort of.

What happened to it?

It's dumb.

Tell me.

Ben needed to know.

It's *really* dumb.

Flegg was embarrassed, Ben could see. But he needed to know what had happened. He *deserved* to. "Tell me!"

"I ate it."

"*What?* Why?" Ben wasn't chuckling, but he wanted to.

"Mom always says you are what you eat. When the fortune didn't work like it was supposed to, I figured maybe I had to eat it first, like I ate the other ones. Like I said, it's dumb."

"You're not *dumb,* Flegg," said Ben. "Maybe you're onto something, actually. I think the fortune *might be* working."

"What do you mean?" Flegg sounded hopeful.

"I mean maybe the fortune didn't give me a scooter because scooters aren't actually the *best* things. And neither are Mega Megas."

"Then what *are*?" Flegg leaned forward like he really *needed* to know.

Ben wasn't sure what the best things were, but he listened to his *thump*ing heart and made his best guess.

"Other people, I think. People who make you laugh or teach you stuff. People who show up when you ask them to. People who give you their last three dollars."

Flegg shook his head.

People don't like me. That's why I take their cookies.

FLEGG	PEOPLE
TOOK COOKIE	DON'T LIKE ME
DID NOT TAKE COOKIE	STILL DON'T LIKE ME

That logic didn't work for Ben. "People might like you better if you *didn't* take their cookies, Flegg."

"They still wouldn't like me." Flegg shook his head again. He was sure.

But Flegg was wrong. Ben wanted to prove it. "That kid whose ball you got out of the tree. Noah. *He* likes you."

Flegg didn't say anything, but Ben could tell he was thinking about it.

"Why did you do that, anyway?" Ben asked.

"Because," said Flegg matter-of-factly, "his ball was stuck in the tree."

In that moment, Ben saw it. Flegg's *actual* problem. And maybe the actual solution. Flegg *did* understand the Code of the Schoolyard. He just didn't realize it. And how could he? No one had ever bothered to show him how it worked.

Ben had an idea, a way to maybe knock loose
the ball that was stuck in Flegg's own branches.

He reached into his pocket and pulled out his cookie. In the course of his turbulent day, he'd never gotten a chance to eat it.

"Here," he said, handing the cookie to Flegg.

Flegg looked annoyed. "I thought you wanted me to *stop* taking your cookies."

"You're not taking it," Ben argued. "I'm giving it to you. That's totally different."

"What's the catch?" Flegg took the cookie cautiously, as if waiting for it to bite his finger.

"No catch." Ben meant it. He'd never parted with a cookie more willingly.

If Flegg still wanted to steal his cookies after this, Ben wouldn't be able to stop him. But from this point forward, Flegg would always know what it felt like to eat a cookie that someone had wanted to *give* him.

Ben watched as Flegg pulled off
the wrapper and broke the cookie
in two. He popped half into his
mouth and chewed slowly and even
sort of smiled.

And then, instead of eating the
other half, he handed it to Ben.

Here. Have some.
It's good.

Ben took the piece of cookie and popped
it into his mouth.

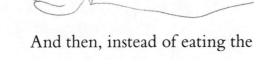

Thanks,
he said, nodding.
It's the *best.*

Ben knew for sure. Flegg
understood. The only thing better
than getting a cookie from someone
else was giving one to them.

"Okay, here goes," said Flegg, holding up the tiny strip of paper. "You ready to hear?"

Ben had forgotten about the fortune! He hadn't gotten a new one in days. Ben knew—*he just knew*—the fortune would explain everything that was currently murky. It would say just what he needed to hear. It would let him know exactly what to do.

Flegg read the fortune aloud.

A journey of a thousand miles begins with a single step.

What? said Ben, taking the fortune and reading it himself.

I *guess* that makes sense, but ...

"Where are we *going*?" asked Flegg, finishing Ben's thought.

"Exactly!" said Ben. "I have no idea."

"That's so far away," said Flegg, who seemed excited by the possibility. "I guess we'd better get started!"

Ben laughed, and then Flegg laughed, and then they laughed together. Whatever journey they were on had already begun.

They sat there a while longer.

The sun was getting lower.

So, can I have my scooter back? asked Flegg.

Yeah, said Ben.

It rides nice.

Doesn't it?

Yeah.

Ben felt good about giving up the scooter, but he didn't want to go back to how things had been. For the two plates to be balanced, things had to actually *change*.

"I'll give it back, but will you—"

"How about I don't take your cookies anymore?" Flegg interrupted.

Ben was surprised. And happy. "That would be great."

"How about I don't take *anyone's* stuff anymore?" It seemed like Flegg was talking to himself.

"Great, but . . . why?" Ben was curious. He didn't want to be suspicious, but he was.

"Isn't that what you want?" Flegg was defensive.

"Yeah, definitely," said Ben. It *was* what he wanted, even more than he wanted an Astrostar. "But I still want to know why you said it."

"Because . . ." Flegg was searching for the right words. "I don't want to anymore."

Ben understood perfectly. When the ball was in the tree, you had to get it out. When it was already on the ground, you could just . . . play.

"Makes sense to me," he said, and they shook on it. Ben worried he might never get his hand back.

It seemed like the kind of truce where both sides give up exactly as much as they get. Which seemed to Ben like a truce that might last.

He and Flegg were never going to be *friends,* not in the way he and Janet were friends. But Ben hoped they were done being enemies.

He got the Astrostar and handed it to Flegg. Then he opened the front door and shouted, "We're finished."

A few moments later, the grown-ups came out.

I've had better tea,

said Flegg's mom.

Helpful to know,

Ben's mom replied.

How are things out here?

asked his dad.

"We're good," said Ben. "The apology was only sort of embarrassing."

"Did you get your scooter back?" Flegg's mom barked.

"Yeah."

"Let's go."

Flegg and his mom got into their truck and backed out of the driveway.

As Ben watched the Astrostar disappear down the road, he felt strangely relieved. He felt light. He felt *free*.

But only for a second.

CHAPTER 31

Ben looked at his mom and dad. Their expressions were not the kind you want to see when you're just starting to feel good about things.

"Ben Yokoyama, why did you take that boy's scooter?" his mom demanded, not actually stomping her foot but seeming like she wanted to.

"*How* did you take that boy's scooter?" Ben's dad was extremely confused and slightly impressed.

"I didn't *take* it. I . . ." Ben wanted to tell the smallest possible lie. "We *traded* for one of my fortunes, but then he changed his mind."

"That's not what his mom said."

"He was afraid to tell his mom what actually happened, so I was covering for him."

"So, you didn't . . . *physically intimidate* him?" Ben's dad wanted details.

"I did not physically intimidate him."

"Okay, then," said Ben's dad. "You're not in trouble for taking his scooter."

"Great," said Ben.

"And you can still use your birthday money to buy a new one." His dad was smiling and proud.

"*About* that," said Ben, who knew it was time to come clean.

Ben's mom gave him a look like a cheese grater gives a hunk of cheddar.

I hope you're not about to say your birthday money is gone.

My birthday money *is* gone,

Ben admitted.

"But only because I used it to support a small woman-owned local business," he added. Ben had often heard his mom talking about the importance of doing just this.

"*Which* woman-owned local business?" Ben's mom was hard to fool.

"You bought *cookies,* you mean?" She was an excellent detective.

"Yes, but I didn't *enjoy* them."

"*Ben.*" She was a human lie detector.

"Okay, I enjoyed them a *little.*"

"*Ben!*"

"They were so delicious I couldn't stop!"

His parents looked at each other. His dad shrugged. His mom sighed. Ben was a pretty good kid overall, and they knew it. His sugar-fueled misdeed was forgivable.

But his mom wasn't quite ready to let him off the hook. "Here's facts," she declared. "We're going to finish making dinner, and you are going to spend some quality time with Dumbles. *Both* of you have some thinking to do."

"What did *Dumbles* do?"

"He refuses to play with his fancy new toys."

"I don't think he—"

"He *likes* them!" Ben's mom growled. "He just doesn't know it yet."

"You did such a great job persuading Flegg to trade you an expensive scooter for a tiny piece of paper," said Ben's dad. "I'm sure you can persuade your dog to play with the Poochinator and Big Rex."

All things considered, it was a reasonable punishment. Ben decided not to press his luck. "Okay," he agreed. "I'll *try*."

They all went inside. Ben's parents headed to the kitchen, and Ben went to the living room, where he found Dumbles stretched out like a dog banana in a warm patch of afternoon sunlight.

Ben picked up the remote control and pressed the button. Big Rex's eyes flashed to life, but Dumbles didn't stir.

Ben amused himself by steering Big Rex around the room, first in looping circles and then in a daring figure eight around the recliner and coffee table. To increase the challenge, Ben drove Big Rex faster and made the circles tighter until—

Big Rex slammed into the coffee table, knocking an empty Chinese takeout container onto the floor.

In one surprisingly acrobatic motion, Dumbles leaped to his feet and pounced on the container, grabbing it with his teeth and tossing it into the air before springing backward in surprise as it landed and clattered and tumbled some more.

As Big Rex lay friendless and glum, Dumbles played with the container like he'd finally unlocked the puppy within.

A few minutes later, he stopped and panted and looked up at Ben with an expression of delirious glee.

"Good boy, Dumbly Doo," said Ben, scratching his dog behind the ears.

After Dumbles caught his breath, he walked across the room and picked up his leash from the basket by the door.

"Should we go for a walk, Dumston?"

Dumbles didn't actually nod, but Ben knew what he wanted, so he grabbed his coat and slipped on his shoes, and they headed outside.

They walked. It was the buttery part of sunset
Ben loved best, when everything was soft and
warm and good like an oven full of cookies or an
extra-heavy quilt on your bed.

It had been a long time, but
they shook off the rust and
remembered how it worked,
Dumbles sniffing bushes and
tree trunks and mailbox posts,
Ben enjoying the easy feeling
of loping slowly down the sidewalk.

They didn't need robot
friends or fancy scooters to
have a nice time. Just the
afternoon light and their very
own feet and . . .

Ben realized something was missing.

He walked to the end of the block and turned right at the corner with the yellow bush. A few minutes later, he rang a familiar doorbell.

The door opened, and there she was, Ben's favorite person in the whole wide world.

"Want to take a walk?"

Sure!

said Janet.

I'll grab my coat.

They walked along together, first one block, and then another, chatting about the day and enjoying the sunset, Ben, Janet, Dumbles, and Coatzilla.

"Do you still have my three dollars?" Janet asked.

Ben reached into his coat pocket, and there were the bills. "Yeah. Do you want them back?"

"Nah," said Janet. "I haven't needed them so far."

Ben thought about it for a second. Neither had he.

They walked and walked. It felt so good that Ben wanted it to last forever. But it was almost time for dinner. "Should we go back?" he asked reluctantly.

Not yet, said Janet with a witchy gleam in her eye.

Just a little bit longer, if you don't mind. I have a feeling we might find some other amazing thing if we just keep looking. I'm really on a roll.

Okay, said Ben.

Whatever you say.

They kept going. But not because Ben was
looking for anything at all.

The best things in life were already his.

And they hadn't cost a penny.

Greetings, friends! My name is Matthew. I wrote this book.

ABOUT THE AUTHOR AND ILLUSTRATOR

And I'm Robbi. I illustrated the heck out of it.

Matthew: Robbi, I wonder if you could help me with something.

Robbi: Sure. You want me to make you an omelet? Give you another haircut? Remind you how great your wife is?

F R E E
is
BEST!

NOT FREE
is
NOT
BEST?

M: Yes to all of that. But first, I need to figure out whether this book is one of the *best things* in life. If someone checks it out of the library, they can read it for "free," so it could be a "best thing." But . . . if they bought it at a bookstore, then it *wasn't* free and *can't* be a "best thing," right?

R: You're overthinking this, my friend. No matter how they got it, this book is one of the best things . . . if our readers *decide* it is. "Best" is a matter of opinion.

M: *This changes everything!* I have so many opinions! And I know you do, too. What do you think the best thing is?

Easy. Picking berries. I could do it all day. And when I find them in the woods, they're *totally* free.

Ugh. You couldn't pay me to pick berries. I hate it when my fingers get sticky. In my opinion, picking berries is the *worst*.

You're entitled to your opinions, but in this case, they happen to be wrong.

R: What do *you* think the best thing is?

M: When Augie* falls asleep on me when we're reading together at night.

Does he charge you for this?

Not yet. But now I'm worried.

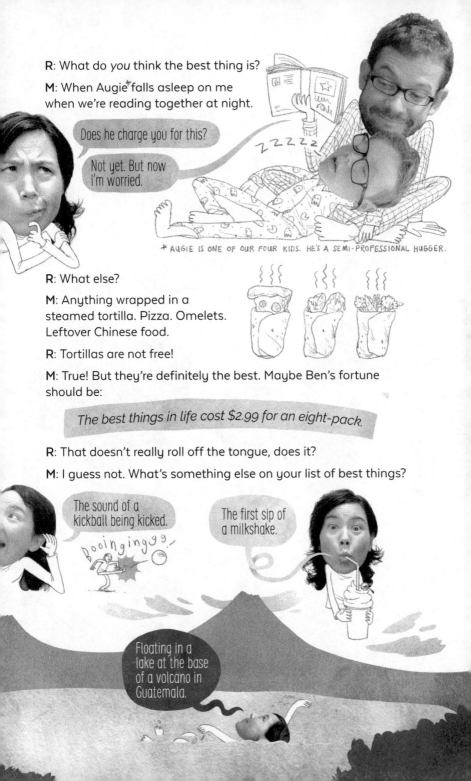

*AUGIE IS ONE OF OUR FOUR KIDS. HE'S A SEMI-PROFESSIONAL HUGGER.

R: What else?

M: Anything wrapped in a steamed tortilla. Pizza. Omelets. Leftover Chinese food.

R: Tortillas are not free!

M: True! But they're definitely the best. Maybe Ben's fortune should be:

The best things in life cost $2.99 for an eight-pack.

R: That doesn't really roll off the tongue, does it?

M: I guess not. What's something else on your list of best things?

The sound of a kickball being kicked.

Boooinginggg!

The first sip of a milkshake.

Floating in a lake at the base of a volcano in Guatemala.

R: *Your turn!*

M: Being married to the person who illustrates my books.

R: I do like making books with you. But it's also one of the *worst* things, because when we're both busy writing and drawing, there's no one to read books to Augie, and he has to fall asleep on himself!

M: Maybe I should charge him for the pleasure of falling asleep on me?

R: Good luck with that.

M: How about you? One more best thing before we go?

Sitting in a raft, watching the salmon jump.

You're right. Watching the salmon is amazing—and doesn't cost anything—but we're usually covered in fish slime, so it can't be the best.＊

＊ WE SPEND OUR SUMMERS RUNNING A SMALL COMMERCIAL SALMON-FISHING OPERATION IN ALASKA

R: I guess you're right. Fish slime is almost as bad as your haircut.

M: You mean the one you gave me yesterday?

R: Yep. It *wasn't* my best work. But . . . it was free!

You get what you pay for, I guess.

R: Whether you buy it at the bookstore or check it out of the library, Cookie Chronicles book 5, *The Cookies of Chaos*, is coming your way soon! And the first three Cookie books are already available.

BOOK 1

BOOK 2

BOOK 3

To find us in the meantime, write us an email, check out our other books, or ask us to come visit your school, library, or conference, by going to:

robbiandmatthew.com

▶ YouTube
Robbi & Matthew

Instagram
@robbi.and.matthew

Or you can find us on YouTube or Instagram, where we post daily videos of Matthew and his amazing wife.

You're the best, Robbi!

That's your opinion.

Maybe so. But in this case, I happen to be right.

HOW THE UNITED STATES GOVERNMENT WORKS

As Rainey will tell you, Honeycutt Elementary is kind of like a tiny version of the United States. Principal Hogan is in charge. The school board makes the rules. And Kid Court makes sure the rules get followed. But a country is slightly more complicated than an elementary school. Here's how the three parts of the American government (we often refer to them as "branches") work together to make things run as smoothly and fairly as possible for everyone—even Flegg.

The **THREE BRANCHES**

THE LEGISLATIVE BRANCH

Makes the laws and decides how much money gets spent on things like bridges, armies, health care, and parades.

AGREED?

YEA!

The Congress is the group of people who actually make the laws. There are two parts of Congress—the Senate and the House of Representatives. Both parts can suggest new laws, but they have to agree before a law gets sent to the president for approval. (Things can get testy.)

Each state also has its own congress—and its own senators and representatives.

DOUBLE YEA!!

FOR EXAMPLE: The U.S. Congress could make a law that says everyone gets one free ice cream cone each day.

THE EXECUTIVE BRANCH

Responsible for approving and carrying out the laws made by Congress.

The President is in charge of this branch. Her job is to think up new laws, pick judges, make partnerships with leaders of other countries, and occasionally pardon turkeys.

Each state has a governor, who is kind of like the president of the state.

The president could approve the free-ice-cream law OR she could veto it (veto means "say no to") because she wants people to get free brownies instead.

THE JUDICIAL BRANCH

Decides who's right and wrong when people disagree, which sometimes means taking a close look at laws and figuring out what they actually mean.

The Supreme Court is made up of nine judges, who are picked by presidents. They can keep their jobs as long as they like. As a result, some of them are extremely wrinkly.

There are many other courts across the country. Because there are lots of people in America, and we tend to disagree a lot.

FOR EXAMPLE: The Supreme Court could overturn the free-ice-cream law because ice cream wasn't mentioned in the Constitution (even though it definitely should have been).

LEGAL SYSTEM BASICS

You've seen how Kid Court works. It's based on the American legal system, which is very complicated and can't be fully described in two pages. But here are some basics* (in case you want to start your own Kid Court or become a Supreme Court justice one day).

LEGAL CASE

A disagreement between two people (or between two towns or between a person and a cup of hot coffee) that may be resolved in court.

Jury: A group of citizens who listen to the case, think about the evidence, and decide whether or not the defendant is guilty.

Defendant: The person accused of doing something wrong. Defendants have to *defend* themselves to prove they're not guilty.

Plaintiff: The person who thinks they have been wronged in some way. The plaintiff has a *complaint*.

Judge: The person who runs the trial and decides what the punishment should be if the jury decides the defendant is guilty. (Such as scraping the gum pole. Ew.)

Evidence: Facts, information, or objects that are shared as part of a trial. (A muddy handkerchief, for example. Or a suspicious trail of cookie crumbs.)

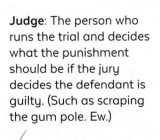

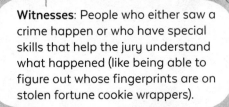

Witnesses: People who either saw a crime happen or who have special skills that help the jury understand what happened (like being able to figure out whose fingerprints are on stolen fortune cookie wrappers).

Lawyers: The people who explain the disagreement to the judge and jury. The lawyers for the plaintiff are called the prosecution, and the lawyers for the defendant are called the defense attorneys.

*If you are a lawyer or a lover of nuance, please hold your nose for now and then write your own book about this.

THE COOKIE CHRONICLES

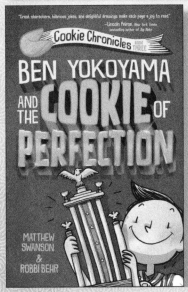

DON'T MISS A SINGLE BITE!

Author-illustrator and husband-wife duo **Matthew Swanson** and **Robbi Behr** are co-creators of the critically acclaimed mystery series the Real McCoys and the picture books *Sunrise Summer, Babies Ruin Everything,* and *Everywhere, Wonder*—in addition to sixty or so self-published books for children and adults. They spend their summers running a commercial salmon-fishing operation on the Alaskan tundra and the rest of the year making books, visiting schools, speaking at conferences, and living in the hayloft of an old barn on the Eastern Shore of Maryland with their four kids and one small dog named Dumbles.

robbiandmatthew.com